Her Amish
Christmas
Sweetheart

Rebecca Kertz

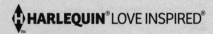

Recycling programs for this product may not exist in your area.

LOVE INSPIRED BOOKS

ISBN-13: 978-0-373-62315-0

Her Amish Christmas Sweetheart

Copyright © 2017 by Rebecca Kertz

www.Harlequin.com

Printed in U.S.A.

"Ready to get started?"

Peter pulled out the chair next to Meg.

"Ja." She tried to act casual with him so near.

"What's that?" He shifted closer and gestured toward the paper before her.

Meg felt her neck tingle. He smelled like soap, outdoors and something uniquely Peter. She'd never been *so* aware of him as a man. "I thought I'd make note of our ideas."

"Gut idea." He glanced up, and there was a jolt as she felt the impact of his gray gaze. "What shall we discuss first? The location? I have an idea that you may like."

"I bet I have a better place," she challenged.

"And where is this *better* place?" he asked with a little smirk. "You haven't heard mine yet."

"Bishop John Fisher's *haus.*"

Peter laughed.

"What's so funny?" she asked, offended.

He sobered instantly. "We came up with the same idea."

Meg blinked. "Honestly?"

"Ja!" They looked at each other and grinned.

"Looks like we've found something we both actually agree on!" Meg was pleased. Maybe this meeting would go smoother than the first one.

Rebecca Kertz was first introduced to the Amish when her husband took a job with an Amish construction crew. She enjoyed watching the Amish foreman's children at play and swapping recipes with his wife. Rebecca resides in Delaware with her husband and dog. She has a strong faith in God and feels blessed to have family nearby. Besides writing, she enjoys reading, doing crafts and visiting Lancaster County.

Books by Rebecca Kertz

Love Inspired

Women of Lancaster County

A Secret Amish Love
Her Amish Christmas Sweetheart

Lancaster County Weddings

Noah's Sweetheart
Jedidiah's Bride
A Wife for Jacob
Elijah and the Widow
Loving Isaac

Lancaster Courtships

The Amish Mother

Be completely humble and gentle;
be patient, bearing with one another in love.
—*Ephesians* 4:2

For Linda C., a wonderful friend
who is generous in spirit and love.

Chapter One

~❦~

November, Lancaster County, Pennsylvania

The Adam Troyer barn was filled to capacity with Amish youth. Young people stood near or sat on benches on both sides of three long tables. Plates with leftovers, snacks and plastic cups with the remnants of iced tea or lemonade littered the tabletops. Meg Stoltzfus and her sister Ellie attended tonight's singing with their friends, including one man from another church district, Reuben Miller, whom Meg had set her eye on from the first moment she met him, over two years ago.

"Ellie," Meg whispered, "Reuben asked to take me home."

"Again?" Ellie teased with a grin.

"Ja." Meg glanced longingly at Reuben. She'd first met him when he and his sister attended a singing at her cousin Eli's invitation, and she hadn't seen him again until three weeks prior, when he'd sought her attention after an unexpected encounter in Whittier's Store.

"Go," Ellie urged, startling her from her thoughts. "You don't want to keep him waiting."

Meg nodded. "I'll be home soon." She turned with a smile, but her good humor vanished as she encountered Peter Zook. She had fallen for him when she was sixteen, and she'd thought they were friends. But she'd been wrong, and she'd found out the hard way after accidently eavesdropping on Peter and his brother. Peter had told Josiah that she was spoiled and in need of discipline. She'd been devastated. Every time she saw him now, she felt her hackles rise.

Determined not to allow him to get to her, Meg smiled politely. "Beautiful night, *ja*, Peter?"

"It's supposed to rain," he said.

She stiffened and turned. "Rain? Honestly, Peter? That's all you have to say?" She fought irritation and won. Her smile became genuine. "Rain or not, I hope you enjoy the rest of your evening." Then she walked to where Reuben waited for her near the door, settling her gaze on him.

"Ready?" Reuben's appreciative smile was a huge boost to her morale as she reached his side. The complete opposite of Peter Zook in looks, Reuben had blond hair and pale blue eyes. Peter, on the other hand, had dark hair and a gaze that was currently a stormy gray.

She froze, then berated herself. Why was she comparing the two men? Why think of Peter at all?

The night was balmy and pleasant as she and Reuben stepped outside. The stars were glistening points of light in a clear, dark sky. *Rain*, Meg thought. *Huh!*

Reuben helped her into his buggy, then climbed onto the seat next to her. She studied him as he picked up the leathers and steered the horse down the dirt lane and onto the main road.

She frowned. What was the matter with her? Reuben

was handsome, kind and good-humored. Yet her joyful mood had dimmed.

Because of Peter Zook. Peter had stolen the fun from her evening.

Meg released a calming breath as she studied the hands that held the reins. She'd felt the calluses on Reuben's fingers when he'd helped her onto the seat. He'd told her recently that he'd been working with a construction company. Strong, hardworking hands. Hands that could belong to a working husband.

Silence surrounded them as Reuben drove the buggy down the dark, deserted road. The only sounds were the clip-clop of horse hooves and the sound of carriage wheels on pavement.

Should she start a conversation? Meg wondered, uneasy with the silence.

"You're quiet," Reuben said softly.

"So are you," she replied with a light laugh.

He turned to regard her with curious eyes. "Did you enjoy the singing?"

"*Ja.* Did you?" She met his light blue eyes, then looked away from the intensity of the gaze.

"I did because you were there."

"That's kind of you to say."

"'Tis the truth." He smiled. She met his eyes again and managed to smile back. "Meg?"

"*Ja*, Reuben?"

"I hope one day soon you'll allow me to court you."

She caught her breath. "You want to court me?" It was what she'd longed for, wasn't it?

"*Ja.*" His lips curved. "I know it's been only a few weeks since we started seeing each other, but I care about you. I can see us having a family together."

She kept silent, unsure what to say. *This is what I*

wanted. Yet despite his willingness to wait, she felt as if he was rushing her into a serious relationship. The image of Peter Zook entered her mind, and she fought to banish it.

"What do you think, Meg? Can you see me in your future? Can you see us marrying and having children together?" He steered his horse into a right turn off the main road.

"This isn't the way to my *haus*," she said, feeling vaguely uneasy.

"*Ja*, I know. I thought I'd take you home the long way." He regarded her warmly as he touched her cheek. "I'm not ready for tonight to end. I want to spend more time with you."

Meg struggled to breathe. "Reuben—"

"Don't worry. I won't pressure you."

She relaxed. "Why me? Why now?"

"I've been working to save money, Meg. I wasn't ready before for a wife and family." He flashed her a tender smile. "I am now. And when I saw you again, I remembered the one evening we spent together, and I just knew. I want you as my wife."

Meg hid her shock. She didn't know how to respond to him. He seemed determined to marry her. And hadn't she always wanted to marry and have children? To prove to her parents that she was strong and would make someone a good wife? And she'd been fixated on Reuben for a long time.

"I'm a patient man," he said softly. "I can wait until you're ready."

As if their wedding were a foregone conclusion. Meg looked out the window, watching the passing scenery. Reuben's confidence bothered her when she should be flattered. She liked him. He was a nice man. But he wasn't what she'd expected.

This is all Peter's fault, she thought bitterly. She'd been trying to recover from her unrequited love for Peter. She'd been foolish enough to be convinced that Reuben was *the one*, despite the fact that she barely knew him. She'd been obsessed with finding him again. Now that he was in her life, she shouldn't be surprised that her feelings for him weren't exactly what she had expected—or hoped for. She should tell him. It wouldn't be right to allow him to hope in vain.

But how would she know that he wasn't the right man for her if she didn't give him a chance?

Clouds in the distance blanketed the sky, covering the stars. It started to drizzle. She scowled. Peter was right. But how could he have possibly known? Within minutes, the drizzle became a mist that coated the roadway and covered the buggy's windshield.

"Is something wrong?" Reuben asked.

She bit her lip. Should she explain how she was feeling? *Give him a chance.* "*Nay*, but I—" A car came around a corner too fast and sideswiped the buggy, forcing the horse off the road. "Reuben!" she screamed.

Meg anticipated her death as the animal reared up on its hind legs and then bolted, dragging the vehicle down an embankment. Pain reverberated in her head as it slammed against the carriage's sidewall. She felt a jerk, then the buggy tilted and rolled. Her body lurched painfully as it continued to tumble down the hill.

The pitching stopped suddenly with a splash. Searing agony and cold wetness enveloped her just before she blacked out.

Peter watched Meg leave with a sick heart. Even after all these years, he couldn't forget what she'd said to him after she'd overheard him talking with his brother about her. He'd been mortified to realize that she'd heard him speak of his feelings for her—and she'd been upset by it. He'd thought they were friends, and he'd hoped for more. Even if she hadn't returned his love, she could have let him down gently, he thought bitterly. Instead, she'd been angry and spoken scathingly to him.

"I overheard what you told your *bruder*, Peter Zook!" she'd snapped. "You have some nerve. I thought I knew you, but I was wrong. From now on, stay away from me! *Just leave me alone!*"

Yet despite her hurtful words, he'd been foolish enough to hope things between them would eventually change, so he'd been prepared to wait. After all, she'd been only sixteen. He'd hoped that with maturity they would come to an understanding, and he'd have a chance at winning her heart. But it would never happen now. Meg finally had the man she wanted—and it wasn't and would never be him. What was it about her that wouldn't let him move on and forget her?

Peter scowled. He knew she'd obsessed over Reuben, but he'd figured it was only a matter of time before Meg realized that she'd been infatuated with a memory. But now everything had changed, with Reuben's return to Meg's life. The man obviously reciprocated her affection.

His stomach clenched painfully. He couldn't stand seeing her with Reuben. He should have tried harder to become friends with her again, but he'd hoped that if he stood back, watched and waited, she'd eventually soften toward him.

I've been too patient. I've waited too long. Years before that awful day she'd spurned his love, he should have tried to woo her.

She wants nothing to do with me. He needed to forget about her and move on. He needed to wed soon. His father was getting too old to farm, and with Josiah married and living elsewhere, it was up to Peter to take over the family farmhouse. Once he married, his parents would move into the *dawdi haus* on the property where Grandfather and Grandmother Hershberger had lived before they'd passed on. His father had mentioned several times in the last month wanting to move. An accident years ago had left his *dat* with a severely broken leg, which still pained him on occasion.

Peter wanted his parents to be happy. He knew they were upset because his sister Barbara hadn't been home in over a year. Knowing his father would be delighted by the plan, Peter firmed his resolve to find a woman to marry before November of next year, the time for Amish weddings.

There were other girls within his community. Nice girls. Young women who seemed to like him. He would find a new love to marry. Someone like his good friend Agnes Beiler. Lately he'd glimpsed something in her gaze that hinted she was open to more than friendship with him.

Unfortunately, he would be working with Meg Stoltzfus in the coming weeks till Christmas, whether he wanted to or not. This morning his father had approached him and asked that he help with a surprise party for his mother. His *mam's* birthday was on Christmas Day—and so was Meg's father's. His *dat* and Meg's *mam* wanted the two of them to plan a joint surprise birthday party. He once would have looked forward to spending time with her, when he'd still had hopes of winning her heart. But not now. Planning a party with her was the last thing he wanted—or needed.

Perhaps he worried needlessly. Meg might refuse to work with him, and he'd be off the hook.

Yet how could he deny his mother a birthday party? His *mam's* father—his *grossdaddi*—had died several months ago, and *Grossmammi* had followed him to the grave less than a week later. It had been a terrible time for his *mam* and family. While his mother had a strong belief that her parents were with the Lord, *Mam* still felt the pain of her loss.

So he would work with Meg if it meant bringing a glimmer of happiness into his mother's life. *Mam* was a wonderful wife and mother, and Peter would not fail in the task his father had assigned him. Whether or not Meg wanted it, they would plan a party together that neither parent would forget.

Forcing Meg from his thoughts, he approached his friend. Agnes Beiler was a kind girl with an inherent sweetness. With the singing over, he decided to offer her a ride home. Although Agnes lived in the next church district, he figured he could manage the distance from the Troyer farm to the Beiler residence in a reasonable amount of time before heading home. Peter studied her, enjoying the view, anticipating taking their friendship to the next level. It just made solid sense to fall for a good friend. Friendship was a good basis for marriage.

He leaned close and softly asked, "Agnes, may I take you and your sister home?"

She beamed at him. "*Ja.* That would be *wunderbor*, Peter. Just let me tell Alice."

He watched her approach her sister, who briefly glanced in his direction and then nodded. He saw Agnes move to her younger brother, who had brought the girls. The sisters then headed in his direction, clearly delighted for him to take them home. A mental image of

Meg intruded, but he banished it. Agnes was just the person to get her out of his thoughts—and his heart.

The young women reached him. He grinned. "All set?"

"*Ja.* Are you sure you don't mind?" Agnes had likely suspected his feelings for Meg, and her eyes were sympathetic as she gazed at him.

"*Nay,* I'm more than happy to take you." He regarded her with warmth, and was pleased to see Agnes's eyes light up and her lips curve with pleasure. He assisted the sisters into the open buggy and then steered the horse toward the Joshua Beiler farm. The ride went quickly. It started to drizzle as he helped the sisters from the vehicle.

"I'll see you again soon." Agnes hurried toward the house after her sister, then waved from the front stoop.

As he headed for home, Peter brightened at the possibility of a new, meaningful relationship with Agnes. There were no streetlights and the road was dark. Rain, which began as a mist, fell in earnest, and he had to watch carefully. The family buggy would have offered him some protection from the rain, but his parents had taken it to his sister Annie's for a light supper. Unfortunately, he'd forgotten to put back the umbrella usually stored under the wagon seat after Annie had returned it last week.

Water pooled on the brim of his Sunday best black felt hat and ran in rivulets down his back. A light wind gust tossed the rain into his face, and he used his sleeve to wipe his eyes. He would be soaked before he got home, but there was no getting around it. He caught sight of an Amish buggy's running lights directly ahead on his side of the road. The headlights of an oncoming car blinded him for a second and then veered. Peter watched with growing horror as the car took the turn too fast and struck the vehicle ahead of him. The horse reared up and ran off the road. His eyes widened as the carriage rolled, out of control, and the car raced past him.

Stunned, Peter spurred his horse into a canter. His heartbeat thundered in his chest when he spied the buggy upended on the far side of the creek. After braking, reining in and finally securing his horse to a tree, he tossed his hat on the ground and ran to the water's edge. Only to find Reuben Miller lying near the edge of the stream.

Peter ran to him. "Reuben! Are you *oll recht*?" He gently shook him. "Reuben!"

"Meg." His gaze unfocused, Reuben attempted to sit up, grimaced, then fell back and closed his eyes. The man had been thrown from the vehicle.

"Meg is with you?" Peter asked, overcome with sudden stark terror. This wasn't the road to the Arlin Stoltzfus farm!

Reuben groaned. "Meg."

"Meg!" The rain fell in earnest as Peter waded into the water toward the overturned buggy. By some miracle, the horse had broken free when the vehicle had overturned, and now stood several yards away, a piece of the damaged harness still attached to it. *"Meg!"*

The water was deeper than he'd thought. He held his breath and dived under. He panicked when he didn't see her. Gasping, he shot up for air, then, frantic to find her, went under again. Adrenaline rushed through him, allowing him to stay underwater longer. His lungs hurt, in need of oxygen, and he lunged up to the surface once more. And then he saw Meg, several feet away. Faceup, but submerged in water, her dark hair floating about her eerily, her legs wedged under the damaged vehicle. His throat tightened as he battled fear.

Meg! He drew a deep breath and swam underwater until he was by her side. He reached out a hand, grabbed her arm and gently tugged. His heart thundered with gratitude as he was able to pull her legs from under the buggy. *Please, Lord, let her be well.* He continued to silently pray for her.

Finally, he had her close, and he raised her head above the water as he swam with her to the shallows, where he could stand. Then he swung her up into his arms and cradled her against his chest as he carried her to land.

Emotion lurched within his chest as he tenderly brushed back wet strands of dark hair from her unusually pale face. He set her gently on the ground close to Reuben. *Please, Father, help me help her. I'll leave her alone. I'll move on with my life. Please just let her live!*

He knelt beside Meg. When he saw that she wasn't breathing, his blood ran cold. Peter turned her onto her belly, then pressed down on her back several times in a steady rhythm. When she didn't respond, he turned her over again, tilted her head back and bent to give her mouth-to-mouth. Her lips were soft but cold. As he drew breath, then blew air into her lungs, he felt his fear escalate, but he remained focused as he worked to save her life. He stopped the breaths to press his hands below her sternum a few times, then continued mouth-to-mouth. He prayed he was doing correctly what he'd learned from a first-aid course.

Meg sputtered and gagged. Dizzy with relief, Peter quickly turned her over yet again, and with his arm beneath her shoulders, held her up as she vomited water. Tears filled his eyes as she coughed, then took several rough, gasping breaths. He waited until she quieted, then eased her onto her back. When he saw that she was breathing normally again, he offered up a silent prayer of thanks. Then he moved to check on Reuben.

"Reuben, I'm going to get help. Meg is right here next to you."

The man groaned.

"Reuben, do you understand? Meg is *oll recht*." He hoped and prayed it was true.

When Reuben didn't answer, Peter raced up to the road. As a vehicle approached, he waved his arms and shouted, but the driver zipped by. This section of road was dark and lonely, and he feared he'd be unable to get Meg and Reuben the medical attention they needed. He caught sight of another car. This time he ran into the road to flag it down, and prayed the driver would stop in time to avoid hitting him.

The car slowed. Peter moved off the road as the vehicle pulled next to him, and someone rolled down the passenger window. It was a middle-aged couple, the man in the driver's seat.

"Do you need help?" the woman asked.

"Yes," he said. "Do you have a phone?" When she said she did, he asked, "Would you call for medical assistance? There's been an accident. My friends—they're down by the creek."

The man parked his car while the woman dialed emergency services. Peter paced, anxious to get Meg and Reuben the help they needed.

Meg's near drowning had flattened him. He'd managed to save her, but what if she'd been underwater too long? He wanted her to be all right. He loved her. He closed his eyes and sent up another prayer.

The woman stepped out of the car, drawing his attention. "An ambulance is on its way."

"Thank you," Peter said.

Within minutes, the ambulance arrived, and he watched helplessly as the paramedics rushed toward the creek. He saw them examine Reuben and Meg before carefully lifting Meg onto a stretcher. The EMTs carried her up the incline to the road. A second ambulance arrived on the scene, and the medics hurried toward Reuben.

Peter approached Meg's stretcher. "Is she all right?"

"We'll know more after the doctor examines her in the hospital." The EMT gazed at Peter through narrowed eyes. "You know her?"

"*Ja*, we belong to the same church," he said. After a brief hesitation, he added, "My sister is married to her cousin."

Peter stared with concern as they carried the stretcher toward the ambulance. To his shock, Meg's eyelids flickered without opening. "Reuben?" she said.

The technician met his gaze. Peter gestured toward the stretcher currently being carried up from the water's edge. The man nodded with understanding.

"He's getting medical attention," the technician told her.

Meg didn't open her eyes. *"Oll recht?"*

Peter's heart thumped hard as he studied her. "She asked if he is all right," he told the EMT.

"He's awake and responding," the man said. "He'll be taken to the hospital for a complete checkup." He and his coworker hefted Meg's stretcher into the ambulance.

The other workers carried Reuben toward the second emergency vehicle. Peter approached it. "I'll get word to his family." The EMT nodded.

"Meg?" Reuben muttered.

"She's on her way to the hospital," he said. "She asked about you." He felt a pang when Reuben sighed and closed his eyes.

Peter stepped back and watched while the EMTs entered their vehicles and started their engines. He felt chilled as he stood in the heavy downpour as the ambulances left. *Lord, please help her.* He stared at the vehicles' bright, multicolored flashing lights as they dimmed with distance, then disappeared from sight. He retrieved Reuben's horse, tied it to the back of his buggy and headed toward the Miller farm to return the animal.

Chapter Two

Meg woke up in pain. Even with her eyes closed, she could tell by the familiar antiseptic smell that she was in the hospital. Her head hurt, but the heavy weight bearing down on her leg felt worse. She shifted and moaned as pain permeated every inch of her body. She opened her eyes and tried to sit up, then gasped at the searing agony in her left leg. She lay whimpering as she prayed for relief. *Make it stop. Please, Lord, make it stop!* Tears spilled down her cheeks as she continued to suffer.

"Meg?" a familiar voice said.

A face loomed in her line of vision as she opened her eyes. "Nell?"

"*Ja, schweschter.* How are you feeling?"

"Awful. I hurt everywhere, especially my leg." She turned her head to meet her sister's gaze and groaned. The simple movement had hurt.

"Hold on, Meg. I'll get help." Then Nell disappeared.

"Nell!" She felt alone and scared. How badly was she injured?

Her sister wasn't gone long. "Meg, I've brought a nurse. She'll give you something for the pain."

"What happened?"

Nell, who'd been watching the nurse insert a needle into Meg's IV, glanced at her with concern. "You don't remember?"

"Nay."

"You were in an accident last night. You and Reuben. He was driving you home when a car struck his buggy and forced it from the road."

It had been raining. She recalled the terror she'd felt as she saw the car's headlights, felt the horse rear and the buggy pick up speed as it upended and rolled. She'd felt a searing pain, heard the splash of cold water before it enveloped her—and then nothing. "I remember now." She felt drowsy all of a sudden, and her pain eased. "Is he *oll recht*?"

"Reuben?" Nell asked.

"Ja." She had a vague impression of hearing someone's voice after the accident. "How did I get here?"

"By ambulance. Reuben did, too. You have a concussion and some bruising." She hesitated. "Your left leg is broken."

Meg shifted and suddenly realized that the heavy weight on her leg was a cast. Her breath hitched. "How bad is Reuben hurt?"

"He fared better than you. He has some bumps and bruises, as well as a concussion, but no broken limbs."

"Is he here?" Meg asked drowsily.

"Ja, in a room down the hall. The nurse told me he'll be released today." Nell grew quiet. "You nearly drowned. Reuben pulled you out of the water. He saved your life."

A man she could rely on, she thought. Meg shivered. "The water was so cold." She got chilled just thinking about it. "I'm so tired." She fought to keep her eyes open.

"'Tis the pain medication. Rest." Her sister covered her with another blanket.

The warmth and the weight made her sigh. "Where's *Dat* and *Mam*?"

"Downstairs eating breakfast. I sent our sisters home. Everyone has been here all night. They didn't want to leave, but I insisted."

"Gut," she murmured sleepily. *"Danki*, Nell." She managed to open one eye. "You're newly married. You shouldn't be here."

"Don't you worry. James isn't far. Sleep, Meg. We'll be here when you wake up."

Almost immediately, Meg drifted into sleep. When she next opened her eyes, she saw that she had slept for some time, for the light came through the window from a different angle. She tried to rise and cried out. Her leg throbbed as she fell back again.

Her father bolted up out of a chair near her bedside, drawing her attention. "Meg, *dochter*, you want to sit up?"

"Dat." She blinked back tears. "I want to, but it hurts too much when I try."

He reached toward the side of her bed. "I'm going to raise your head some. Tell me if it hurts."

Her bed rose slowly, and while Meg felt the movement, the shift didn't cause terrible pain. "That's *gut*." She managed a smile. *"Danki."*

He nodded and stepped back to examine her carefully. "I'm glad you're awake. We've been worried."

"I'm sorry, *Dat*." She could only imagine what her family must have felt after receiving news of the accident.

"Not your fault," her father said with a slight smile. "All that matters is that you're alive and will recover."

"*Ja*, I'll be fine." She studied his tired features with concern. It looked as if he had aged several years in one night. The knowledge that it was her fault upset her. "You should go home and rest. Nell said you were here all night."

"You were in an accident. Where else would I be but by your side?"

"And now it's time for you to go home."

He waved her suggestion aside. "Not yet."

She worried that the accident would cause him to be more protective of her than he already was. Ever since her last hospital stay, he'd tried to shelter her from every little thing. Fortunately, during the past two years, she'd been able to stand up to him a bit, and he'd finally learned to relax. Now her new injuries would take away that freedom she'd fought so hard for.

"Nell said that Reuben is *oll recht*."

Dat nodded. "He'll be discharged today. He wants to stop in to see you before he leaves."

Her mother came into the room. "Meg!" She hurried toward the bed. "You're awake."

Meg managed to grin. *"Ja, Mam."*

Nell entered next, and then James, her husband of just over a week.

"Meg, it's good to see you awake and smiling," her brother-in-law said.

"I told you we wouldn't be far." Nell eyed her closely, her gaze sharp. "How are you feeling? Still in pain?"

"A little, but not it's not as bad as before," Meg assured her. "How long did I sleep?"

"Four hours," her father said.

Meg was alarmed. "Four hours!"

"You needed the rest," her mother murmured soothingly.

Her injuries had kept her family from their beds, and she felt guilty. "Please go home. I'll be fine. You all need to sleep." She captured her father's gaze. "Please, *Dat*?"

"We'll go, but we'll be back to visit this evening," her father said.

"Tomorrow is soon enough," Meg insisted. "You can't be traveling back and forth. 'Tis too much." She bit her lip then winced. "Is every part of me bruised?"

"Nay," Mam said too quickly.

Meg offered a lopsided smile. "I bet I have a black eye." She saw the truth in her father's gaze. Things could have been much worse, she realized. She recalled her last time in the hospital, when a ruptured appendix had nearly caused her death. Some bruises and a broken bone would heal.

"You don't look bad," Nell said.

Meg snorted. "It doesn't matter how awful I look when there is nothing I can do about it." She studied her family, recognizing the exhaustion caused by their night of worry and fear. "I love you all, but go home. I'll be fine." She held up the nurse-call button. "I have everything I need."

Reuben came into the room, but stopped abruptly when he saw her family.

Dat glanced at the young man. "We should leave."

"Please don't leave on my account," he said.

"They're leaving because of me," Meg explained, her lips curving. "I told them to go." She looked at her father. "They haven't slept."

Reuben approached the end of her bed. He froze when her father placed a hand on his shoulder. *"Danki* for saving her," *Dat* said.

To her amazement, Reuben blushed and looked

slightly uncomfortable. "I…I'm sorry about the accident."

"It wasn't your fault." Her father met her gaze. "We'll see you again soon, *dochter*." He moved to leave, and her family followed.

"Be careful going home," she called out.

Each member of her family murmured quietly to Reuben as they passed him.

"Won't you sit a minute?" she asked softly, as she wondered what they'd said.

Reuben moved quickly then, as if eager to please, and took the seat her father had vacated. "You *oll recht*?"

"I'm fine. No serious injuries." She saw relief settle on his features. She studied him and immediately noted huge bruises on his left cheek and forehead. "Your face… Doesn't it hurt?"

His mouth curved crookedly. "A little. And yours?"

She shrugged, and winced with the simple movement. "I'm achy but I'll survive." She grinned to reassure him.

He studied her with concern. "Meg, I'm sorry—"

She saw regret flicker in his blue eyes. "*Nay! Dat's* right. It wasn't your fault. The car hit *us*."

He sighed. "I'm afraid I'm a little foggy about what happened."

Meg was concerned. "You don't remember anything?"

"I recall a blinding light."

"The car's headlights."

He nodded. "The car hit my buggy."

Meg regarded him with amusement. "*Ja*, it was traveling too fast around a curve and struck us. Your horse reared up and bolted off the road and then…"

"The buggy rolled," Reuben said hoarsely. "I remember that, but what happened afterward?"

"You must have whacked your head hard."

"Ja." He stood and gently took hold of her hand. "You must have, too." He studied her with troubled blue eyes. "Meg, I'd never do anything to hurt you intentionally."

The man was sweet, and she was grateful that he'd saved her life. She felt a wave of warm gratitude toward him. "I know."

He didn't move. He simply held her hand and gazed at her with affection that made her feel increasingly uncomfortable. He smiled and toyed with her fingers until Meg closed her eyes and silently prayed that he'd leave.

Peter couldn't get Meg out of his mind. Which was why he drove the two hours to the hospital to make sure she was all right. He parked his buggy near a hitching post, tied up his horse, then hurried inside to the information desk. "Can you tell me where to find Meg Stoltzfus? She's a patient."

The woman behind the counter searched the computer on her desk. "Room 202," she said. "The stairs are to the right. The elevator is farther down the hall."

"Thank you." Peter ran up the stairs to the second floor and followed the signs that led him to Meg's room. His heart started to beat rapidly as he heard voices. He hesitated at the door, then peeked inside—and froze when he saw Reuben Miller at Meg's bedside. The man's face was bruised, but he was smiling affectionately at Meg as he held her hand.

Peter quietly backed away from the room and headed downstairs, his heart aching at the sight of them together. His first instinct was to go home, but then he thought better of it. He had come all this way to make sure Meg was all right. He refused to leave without talking with her. She wouldn't be glad to see him, but he couldn't care less. He needed to know if he'd caused her serious injury when he'd pulled her from the water.

It was well past noon, and he was hungry. He hadn't eaten since an early breakfast. He'd grab something from the hospital cafeteria before he returned to Meg's. If Reuben was still there, he'd go ahead and visit her, anyway. But he preferred to see Meg alone.

After lunch, he took the elevator back to her room. He paused before entering. Meg lay in bed, staring out the window as if lost in thought. She was alone. He stepped inside, and as if sensing him, she turned.

"Peter."

"*Hallo*, Meg." He approached, noting a myriad of expressions crossing her face. He sucked in his breath as he studied her. There were bruises on her forehead and left cheek, and around her left eye. Had he done that to her? "How are you feeling?"

Her lips twisted in a lopsided smile. "I've been better."

He nodded, taking in every inch of her features. Even battered and bruised, she was still the prettiest girl he'd ever known. "I... How bad are your injuries?"

"Is your family here?"

"*Nay*, I came alone."

"What are you doing here?" she asked abruptly, and he tried not to flinch. Would it always be this way between them?

She released a sharp breath. "I'm sorry. I'm feeling out of sorts, but there is no need for me to be rude."

Peter cocked an eyebrow but didn't say anything. Meg flushed, and he softened his expression. "You're in pain. Do you want the nurse?"

Relief settled on her features. "*Nay*, I'm *oll recht*. My leg aches, but I'll live."

His gaze fell on the bedcovers, identifying the lump beneath them. "You broke your leg." Did she break it when he'd pulled her from under the buggy? His belly burned at the thought.

"*Ja.* That's what hurts the most."

"Is there anything I can do for you?"

She looked stunned by his concern. "I… Peter, I appreciate your concern but—"

"You don't want it."

To his shock, she shook her head. "I don't deserve it." She looked away. "I haven't exactly been nice to you."

He shrugged. "As I recall, you were very polite the night of the singing, before you left." He paused. "I was rude."

"You warned me about the rain." She shifted in bed, and he saw her wince at the slight movement. "I don't know how you knew."

"*Ja*, well, I have a confession to make," he said. Curiosity entered her blue eyes as she waited for him to finish. His lips twisted. "I didn't know it was going to rain when I said it. I was just…" He couldn't continue. The knowledge that he'd said it simply to ruin her night made him feel small and ashamed.

To his surprise, Meg laughed.

He stared at her, then found himself grinning. "I'm glad you think it's funny."

"I didn't then, but I do now. I guess the accident put things into perspective for me."

Peter stared at her, mesmerized by her bright azure eyes, one sporting a black bruise. Something kicked in his gut as he studied her. If only things could be different between them. But he reminded himself that she was in love with Reuben, and he had Agnes now. "I'm sorry you went through that."

Her eyelashes flickered. "You sound sincere."

"Have I been so terrible to you?" he asked quietly. When she opened her mouth and then promptly closed it, he said, "I see."

"Peter."

"'Tis fine, Meg. I understand." He shifted on his feet. "I'm sorry if what I said hurt you." He was referring to when she was sixteen and hadn't lived long in Happiness. "I'd hoped that after all this time, we could be friends." He couldn't read her demeanor. When she didn't respond, he sighed. "You need your rest. I should leave." He started toward the door, then stopped. "How is Reuben? Is he *oll recht*?" he asked, not wanting to give away that he'd seen the two of them together.

Meg's expression warmed. "He's well. He's been discharged." She studied her hands as if her fingers were fascinating. "Did you know that he rescued me? He pulled me out of the water." She rubbed the side of her face where another bruise had formed.

"I hadn't heard." Something jolted in Peter's chest, but he didn't refute her statement. It didn't matter that it was he and not Reuben who had rescued her. The only thing that mattered was that Meg was alive and well, and on the road to recovery. "He must be glad he was able to help you," he said carefully.

"I suppose." She frowned. "When I thanked him, he seemed uncomfortable, as if he didn't feel like a hero." She looked thoughtful. "He told me he doesn't remember what happened after the accident."

Peter nodded in understanding. Reuben obviously felt uncomfortable because he couldn't recall pulling Meg from the creek. "He hit his head?"

"*Ja*, he has a concussion." She closed her eyes for a moment before opening them again.

"Yet they are sending him home and keeping you here," he murmured.

"Just until tomorrow. Then I'll be released." She gestured toward her IV. "They're pumping me with antibiotics to prevent infection in my lungs."

"That makes sense." He saw her eyes drift shut and he stepped back. "I'll be heading home. Is there anything I can do for you before I go?"

Eyes closed, she shook her head.

"Get well, Meg," he said softly.

Her eyelashes flickered before she looked at him. "*Danki*, Peter," she murmured. "It was nice of you to come."

"Take care of yourself," Peter said, before he turned and left—and fought the urge to glance back. Seeing her again made it difficult to forget her…and how much he'd loved her.

As he climbed into his buggy minutes later, he had a sudden longing to see Agnes. He'd drive over to her family's farm before heading home. Because it was suddenly imperative that he see her today.

Chapter Three

"Are you ready to go?" Meg's *dat* asked as he entered her room.

Rick Martin, their English neighbor, was there to take them home. Grabbing her crutches, Meg rose on her one good foot. "I'm ready," she said softly. She glanced toward the door behind her father. "Where's *Mam*?"

"She's giving the nurses the apple pies she baked for them."

"How many?" Meg asked.

Her father shrugged. "Four."

She laughed, feeling warmth for her thoughtful mother. "I wish I could have seen the looks on their faces when she gave them the pies."

As she and her father left her room, Meg caught sight of her mother chatting with the women in the nurses' station.

"Mam," she said as she approached.

"Gut," Mam said. "We can finally get you home."

Nurse Nancy went for a wheelchair. When she returned, she helped Meg get seated and then gave her final instructions on the antibiotic medicine that she'd be taking for the next ten days at home, along with a slip of paper with appointment details for a follow-up with the doctor. Nancy rolled the wheelchair toward the elevator, which opened as they drew near. Meg was surprised to see her sister emerge.

"Look who I found downstairs!" Ellie exclaimed.

"It's the young man who came to see if you were all right yesterday," Nancy said.

Meg immediately thought of Peter, until Reuben stepped out of the elevator behind Ellie. Looking handsome despite the bruises on his cheek and forehead, he approached.

"I heard you were going home today." His blue eyes warmed as he studied her. "I wanted to see you before you left. I hope you don't mind."

"We're glad you came," *Mam* assured him, and Meg could hear warmth in her mother's voice.

Reuben chatted as he accompanied them to the ground floor and then to the car. Meg vaguely heard what he said. For some reason, all she could think about was Peter's visit to her hospital room yesterday. Had he really come because he was concerned? What had he heard that made him travel all this way just to see her?

Whatever his reason, she was surprised and a little pleased that he'd taken the time to visit her. Ellie had urged her to figure out a way for them to get along. From what he'd said, Peter wanted the same thing. If not for Reuben, she would have died from the accident. *Life is too short to hold a grudge.* Surely she could put the past where it belonged, and forgive and forget what he'd said.

After he walked them to Rick's car, Reuben left, after promising to visit her later in the week. Once home, her father thanked Rick for driving them, then helped

Meg into a chair in their great room and then grabbed a cushioned stool to rest her leg on.

"Danki." She sat back and closed her eyes…and soon drifted to sleep.

Meg woke sometime later. She didn't think she'd slept long, judging by the sunlight shining through the great room windows. Her leg hurt, and she shifted in the chair to find a better position just as her youngest sister, Charlie, entered the room.

"Meg!" she exclaimed. "You're awake. I've been wanting to talk with you. I'm sorry I didn't get back to the hospital before you came home."

Her sister's boundless energy was evident in her sparkling green eyes. Charlie pulled a chair close and studied Meg.

"Charlotte May," her mother said as she entered the room. "Did you wake up your sister?"

"Nay, Mam. She was already awake."

"She needs her rest. Run along and finish your chores." As Charlie left, *Mam* turned to her. "Do you think you'll feel well enough to come on visiting Sunday? We'll be going to Aunt Katie's."

Meg hesitated. Would she be able to manage a day's outing? Learning to use the crutches had exhausted her. She could find a chair and stay seated, she supposed. And she certainly wouldn't mind seeing her Lapp cousins and church community friends.

"Your *vadder* is borrowing a wheelchair for you to use while you recover," *Mam* said. "You might find it easier to move about."

Meg nodded. "That's thoughtful of him."

Her mother looked relieved. Meg realized her family would stay home if she wasn't up to visiting, and she became more determined than ever to show them that she was strong despite her recent hospital stay.

"There is something I need to discuss with you." *Mam* glanced briefly toward the kitchen once they were alone.

Meg eyed her with concern. "Are you *oll recht*?"

Her mother gazed at her with warmth. "I'm fine." She grabbed a wooden chair and set it to face her daughter's.

"Mam?"

"There is something I need you to do for me, Meg. You know that your *dat's* birthday will be here soon."

"Ja, on Christmas."

"Ja." She shifted her chair closer, indicating she wanted to speak in private. "I'd like to surprise him with a birthday party," she said quietly. "I've had a conversation with Horseshoe Joe. Did you know that Miriam's birthday is the same day as *Dat's*?"

"Nay, I didn't." Meg got a funny feeling inside.

"Joe wants to give Miriam a party, too. We've decided that we'd like you and Peter to plan one together."

Meg found it difficult to breathe. "You want me… and Peter to work together?"

"Ja, and before you say a word, Meg, I'd like to remind you that you have a broken leg and can't do chores. This celebration is important to me and to Horseshoe Joe. The best people for this task are you and Peter. You'll work with him, *ja*?"

Meg, in fact, had been ready to object to the arrangement, but she wisely kept silent. Her mother was right. She couldn't do chores while her leg was healing. Working with Peter so her father and his mother could have a surprise birthday celebration was something she could do to be useful. "I'll be happy to work with Peter to plan the party."

"Wunderbor!" Mam rose and put her chair back where it belonged. "You mustn't tell a soul. Not even your sisters. Do you understand?"

Meg nodded.

"Gut." Her mother looked pleased. "Lunch will be ready in a minute. Do you need help getting to the kitchen?"

Meg shook her head. *"Nay.* I'll be there in a minute." Her mother left her alone with her thoughts. She sat a moment and contemplated working secretly with Peter Zook. How would she manage? How would he react to the news?

Yesterday she'd told Peter that the accident caused her to put things in perspective in her life. She sighed. She had to find a way to work with him without her painful past interfering with their working relationship.

She stood, grabbed her crutches and hobbled toward the kitchen. Did Peter already know of their parents' arrangement? Her stomach burned with anxiety. She'd see him tomorrow at her aunt and uncle's. Would she mention the party? Refuse to work with her?

Sunday morning, after a decent night's sleep provided by her pain medication, Meg rose from the bed in the first-floor sewing room. Her sisters, Leah, Ellie and Charlie, were working in the kitchen. Leah was at the stove, cooking eggs. Ellie was setting the table, and Charlie was putting out jars of jams and jellies. Meg had usually been up by six at the latest before the accident, and was shocked that she'd slept until eight thirty. "I'm sorry I slept so late."

"You needed the rest," Leah said with a smile. "Come and eat." She pulled out a chair and helped Meg get situated at the table. "Eggs and toast? Or muffins with jam?"

"A muffin will be fine. Without jam," Meg said, as she reached for a chocolate chip muffin. "Where's *Mam* and *Dat*?"

"*Dat's* outside getting the buggy ready. *Mam's* upstairs."

Meg broke open the muffin and took a bite. "Did *Dat* borrow a wheelchair?"

Ellie set down two cups of tea, one in front of Meg, before she sat across the table from her. "He did. He's already put it in our buggy."

Leah took the chair next to Meg and proceeded to fix her own cup of tea. "Does it bother you? The idea of being in a wheelchair again?"

Meg shook her head. "*Nay.* 'Tis not the same as before." She'd spent several weeks in a wheelchair after she'd been discharged from the hospital, when a ruptured appendix had nearly killed her. A broken leg and a few bruises would heal much faster than severe complications from appendicitis.

After breakfast, her family headed to the Samuel Lapp farm, where Meg saw people she knew gathered around as her father steered their horse into the barnyard. *Dat* parked next to the carriage belonging to her cousin Eli and his wife, Martha. She smiled and waved at them before she saw Horseshoe Joe and Miriam Zook, along with Peter, pull in on their other side. Meg locked gazes with Peter before he climbed out of the vehicle. Then she turned her attention to her father, who reached in to lift her from the back seat.

Meg stood on her good leg as her *dat* went for her wheelchair. She reached to grab the buggy as she teetered there, then struggled for a better handhold. An arm immediately slipped about her waist in support, and she sighed with relief, glad for her sister's help. But the clean, fresh scent of soap and man made her realize that the arm was masculine, strong, and most definitely belonged to Peter Zook. Her heart started to pound as she met his gaze.

"I'm steady now," she assured him, eager for him to move away. Her world tilted, but then righted itself as he released her and stepped back. He turned to leave.

"Peter." He halted and faced her. *"Danki,"* she said softly. Her throat constricted, and she felt her face heat.

Peter eyed her intently and nodded. Then he caught up with his mother and father as they approached the house. Meg watched him go with emotion akin to regret that he hadn't stayed to chat—because she'd chased him away.

Her father moved the wheelchair close to where she stood. "Hold on, and I'll help you."

She felt drained and weak, and was glad to sit. As *Dat* pushed her toward the farmhouse, she started to believe that coming today had been a mistake. She felt tired, shaky…and unsettled by the memory of the warmth and strength of Peter's arm as he'd steadied her.

Peter entered the Lapp house, his thoughts filled with Meg. He'd been fighting the emotion overwhelming him ever since he'd held her in his arms as he'd pulled her from the water.

He spied Agnes across the great room and immediately headed in her direction. His feelings about Meg would surely settle down if he spent time with his friend. *"Hallo,* you," he said, greeting her with a smile.

"Hallo back," she quipped with a crooked grin.

"I didn't expect to see you here." But he was glad she was, if only to take his mind off the sweet scent of Meg's hair and the warmth of her beneath his arm as he'd kept her from falling.

Agnes shrugged. "Katie invited us. She saw my *mudder* at the store."

The Joshua Beilers lived in another church district. Occasionally, they came to church service in the Zooks' community, but not often. Peter had met Agnes after a service last year and they'd become instant friends. Agnes was easy to talk with, and her obvious delight in the world was refreshing. She was the complete opposite of Meg, in looks as well as temperament.

Familiar voices in Katie Lapp's kitchen told him that the Stoltzfus family had entered through the back door of the house.

"Is that Meg?" Agnes asked. "I heard about the accident. How is she?"

He shrugged, pretending indifference. "Fine."

"Let's go see."

"Maybe we should let her get settled in first."

Agnes met his gaze. "I heard she broke her leg."

Peter inclined his head. "*Ja.* She's on crutches." He couldn't forget how she'd looked lying in her hospital bed, bruised, pale and vulnerable.

His brother came into the room, and Peter stared. "Josiah, you came! I haven't seen you in months."

Josiah grinned. He had married Nancy King of the Amos Kings, who lived across the road from Samuel and Katie Lapp. The couple had moved after their marriage, and Peter rarely got to see the two of them. "We came in last night. We're staying with my in-laws. I wanted to surprise *Mam* and *Dat.*"

"Have they seen you?"

His brother nodded. *"Ja."* He grinned, as if delighted by their parents' reaction. Josiah's gaze went to Agnes, who stood silently beside him.

"Sorry," Peter said to both of them. "Agnes, this is my older brother, Josiah. Josiah, meet Agnes Beiler."

The two greeted each other warmly. As Agnes turned to have a word with her twin sister, Josiah shot a pointed glance toward her before raising his eyebrows at Peter.

"We're friends," Peter said, before he could ask.

Josiah nodded. "I saw Meg Stoltzfus." He glanced toward the kitchen with concern. "She was in an accident."

"Ja, Reuben Miller was taking her home from last week's singing when a car hit his buggy and forced it from the road."

"Anything serious?" his brother inquired. "I didn't want to ask."

"Worst of it is a broken leg."

"You two getting along yet?"

"We're…polite." Peter had told his brother about Meg overhearing their conversation. His brother had understood and been sympathetic. "She's with Reuben Miller now."

"And you have Agnes?"

Peter shrugged. "If all goes well."

"There you are," a warm female voice said. His brother smiled as his wife, Nancy, approached. *"Hallo*, Peter."

"Hallo, Nancy," he replied with a grin.

"You knew I wouldn't be far." Josiah regarded his wife with affection. "Weather's too chilly to be outside today."

His brother was lucky to have found a woman to spend his life with, Peter thought.

Elijah, Jedidiah and Jacob Lapp entered the room. "How about a game of baseball?" Elijah suggested. "'Tis cold out, but we'll be warm soon enough."

Martha overheard her husband. "You're going to play baseball outside?" Beside her, his sister Annie pushed Meg's wheelchair.

"They'd better not play inside," Annie retorted.

"Why not?" Jed said. "'Tis not raining."

Elijah's expression softened as he eyed his pregnant wife. "You'll stay inside, *ja*?"

"Why?"

Elijah opened his mouth as if to say something, but quickly shut it again.

"Why should any of us stay inside? We'll watch from the porch." Martha addressed Meg. "What do you say? Are you feeling up to watching your cousins smack a baseball around?"

It was clear that Eli didn't like his wife's decision. Martha was far along with child, and he was clearly concerned about her. "Martha…"

"I'll be fine, husband," she assured him. "Meg?"

"'Tis not like I can stand and watch them," she said with good humor.

Peter studied her with concern. Meg had only recently been released from the hospital. The doctor was treating her with antibiotics to help her lungs stay clear. Would the cold air be bad for her? Wouldn't it be better if she remained inside?

His brother-in-law, Jacob, frowned as he studied his cousin. "Meg, I'll get a blanket for you." He glanced at the other women. "I think you all should have blankets."

"*Gut* thinking." Annie beamed at her husband. "And I'll make us some hot tea."

"Peter?" Jedidiah smiled. "You playing?"

Peter glanced at Agnes, who returned his gaze. "I'll play for a while."

"I can't play long," Noah Lapp, another brother, said as he entered the room. "Food's almost ready."

The men avoided the kitchen entrance and left via the front door of the farmhouse. As they stepped outside, Peter caught sight of the younger Lapp brothers, Isaac, Daniel and Joseph, on the front lawn. Joseph held a ball and bat. Joshua and John King, neighboring boys from across the road, grinned as they all gathered on the dormant grass.

"Who wants to be a team captain?" Peter asked.

There was a good-natured debate as it was decided that Jedidiah and Noah would be captains with the privilege of choosing their teammates. Jedidiah chose Jacob, Peter, Daniel and Joshua. Noah's team was Elijah; Jacob's fraternal twin, Isaac; Joseph and John.

Playing in the outfield first, Peter saw the women emerge from the house and make themselves comfortable on the Lapps' covered front porch. Annie pushed Meg close to the rail, then took the chair next to her. Noah's wife, Rachel, along with Martha and Agnes, joined them, each settling in a rocking chair. Meg remained in her wheelchair with a blanket across her lap.

Peter noted that Agnes sat on the opposite side of the porch from them. She smiled and waved, and he nodded before he returned his attention to the game in time to catch a fly ball hit by Isaac. Jedidiah and his teammates cheered, as did Agnes and Annie.

The game continued. Jedidiah's team exchanged places with Peter, who went up to bat. As he waited for his turn at the plate, Peter glanced toward the porch and captured Meg's gaze. She stared at him without once looking away. His heart beat wildly as he refocused his attention on the game.

"Peter!" Jedidiah called from first base, where he'd landed safely. "You're up!"

He nodded, picked up the bat and slammed the ball across the yard, sending Jedidiah to second base and Jacob to third, before they both continued all the way home.

Katie Lapp stepped outside with her granddaughter Susanna on her hip and her grandson EJ standing next to her. "Food is ready!"

The game ended with a difference of opinion on which team had won, since the score was even, but Jedidiah's team didn't get to finish the inning. The men climbed the porch steps as the women turned to head inside. Martha and Elijah went in together. Agnes chatted with her sister Alice, who stood in the entryway and held the door open until Jedidiah grabbed hold of it. Everyone had entered the house except for Jacob, Annie, Meg and Peter.

"Peter," Annie said. "Will you push Meg's chair inside?"

"Ja." He and Meg gazed at each other. Her eyes widened slightly and her skin flushed red as he turned her chair toward the door.

"You don't have to help me," she said. "I can stand."

"Like you did when you arrived earlier?" he asked as he tipped up the front wheels of the chair and lifted it over the threshold. "Does it bother you to have me help you? You just got out of the hospital, Meg," he said, his voice gruff. "You shouldn't take chances."

Meg stiffened. It felt as if he was poking fun at her near fall earlier. "I don't need your help or a scolding, Peter Zook."

"Meg, I didn't mean—"

When they were inside the entryway, he came around the wheelchair to face her. She was offended by what he'd said. And she thought they could start over and work together on the party?

"*Danki*, Peter. I can manage from here," she said in a tight, dismissive voice. She grabbed hold of her chair's wheels and rolled forward, nearly hitting Peter, who instinctively jumped out of the way. He stared at her, and she flushed with guilt.

"Meg."

She stopped and waited for him to reach her.

Peter sighed. "Are you this difficult with everyone?" he asked. "Or just me?"

Meg refused to answer him. She alternately fumed and fought embarrassment as she wheeled herself into her aunt Katie's kitchen. She was aware that Peter Zook followed closely behind her. She bit her lip to keep herself from telling him to leave her alone. Perhaps she was overreacting. In fact, she probably was, but she was tired, in pain, and wanted nothing more than to go home.

As she rolled her chair into the bright kitchen, where food filled the table and countertops, she felt confused and ill. She shouldn't have come. She should have insisted that her family attend without her. It was too soon after her hospital stay for her to be out and about. She could have been napping or gazing silently out the window at home. Instead, she was aware of Peter behind her, a man who didn't like her. But he'd been thoughtful despite how he felt about her, she realized. Sometimes it seemed as if he could read her mind and gauge exactly how she was feeling.

She sighed. And she'd been rude to him. Again. She'd promised to be a better person. *Please, Lord, help me to be thoughtful and kind to everyone, especially to Peter Zook.*

"Meg." Her mother approached. "I'll fix you a plate."

"*Danki*, but *nay*. I can manage." She was determined to prove that she was fine. As soon as everyone left the room and couldn't watch her, she'd stand up and get some food. Her head and bruises hurt, and her leg throbbed. She looked around but saw no sign of her father or any of the older men. "Where's *Dat*?"

"In the barn," Mae King said. "Most everyone has moved out there."

Meg glanced at the older woman, who was a close friend and neighbor of her aunt's. "They've set up tables?"

"*Ja*," *Mam* said. "Samuel brought in a heater to take away the chill." She settled her gaze on someone behind Meg and smiled. "Peter, here's a plate."

"*Danki*, Missy," he said as he accepted it.

Meg rolled her chair into the corner, out of the way. Refusing to watch Peter while he selected food, she stared at her lap. The quilt that her cousin had gotten for her was done in pretty shades of green and yellow. She was glad it hid her heavy cast. Every time she saw it, she felt helpless and a little afraid.

"Peter." Agnes entered the room and swept past her. Meg watched as the young woman took his plate, then proceeded to fill it for him, with selections from every available cold meat platter, salad and dessert. "Do you want iced tea?"

Meg stared as Peter bent and murmured something in Agnes's ear. She heard her chuckle before Agnes turned toward Meg's aunt with an amused expression.

"Katie," she heard Agnes say, "got any Pepsi?"

"In the back room. Help yourself."

Meg watched as Agnes left. She couldn't keep her gaze from Peter, who had moved into her focus. He stared back, his dark gray eyes unreadable, and she quickly glanced away.

Agnes returned with the glass of cola. "Here you go."

"Missy," Mae King called, "come see what Katie has done to the quilt we've been making."

Her mother slipped from the room. Meg watched Peter and Agnes. The two were smiling, sometimes laughing, clearly enjoying each other's company. Meg blinked back tears. She didn't know why she had the sudden urge to cry. She realized that it had been a long time since she'd felt that free and joyful.

"Meg?"

Startled, she glanced up into Agnes's face. "*Hallo*, Agnes."

"How are you feeling?"

"Sore, but I'll live."

"I'm sorry you were hurt."

Agnes's sharp perusal made her squirm. She didn't want or need the girl's pity. "I'm fine." Meg glanced at Peter, who waited patiently next to Agnes. He eyed Meg intensely, as if he was debating whether or not to say something to her. She looked away.

"Do you need anything?" Agnes asked.

Meg managed a smile. "*Danki*, but *nay*. I appreciate the offer, though."

Her cousin Isaac opened the door and peeked into the room. "Peter, Agnes, are you coming out to the barn?"

"We'll be there soon," Agnes said airily. "Have everything you need, Peter?"

"*Ja, danki,*" he told her warmly.

Agnes gave Meg a sympathetic look. "Take care of yourself."

"I will." Meg watched the couple leave the house. For a moment, she was alone, which was a relief. She should get up and fill a plate, but she wasn't really hungry. She leaned back and closed her eyes.

"Meg."

She gasped and opened her eyes to see a plate of food being thrust in her direction. *Peter.* He was eyeing her with concern. Something warmed inside her. She grew flustered as she realized he'd picked all her favorite foods. *"Danki,"* she whispered. Heart thundering in her chest, she wheeled herself closer to the table.

"Did you want to join us in the barn?"

"I… *Nay.* I think it will be better if I just stay here." She saw him nod, then watched the dark-haired, gray-eyed man depart to rejoin the others. Peter had been thoughtful enough to fill her a plate. The thought made her experience a strange myriad of emotions she couldn't understand. Her face felt warm as she stared at her food. She picked up a fried chicken drumstick and took a bite. It tasted delicious, and suddenly her appetite was back.

She thought of Peter's kindness as she ate every bite of her meal. The man confused and fascinated her. But did he still think as badly of her as he had years before? And if he did, why was he being so nice to her now?

Chapter Four

Peter sat with Agnes on a bench behind a table that Samuel Lapp had constructed using plywood on sawhorses. The girl beside him was chatting with her sister Alice and Meg's sisters Ellie and Charlie. He listened with half an ear, and only fully tuned in when picking up Meg's name during the conversation.

"She's *oll recht*?" Agnes asked, her expression filled with concern.

"Meg's tough," Ellie said. "She'll be fine in a week or so."

"She looks bad, though, doesn't she?" Meg's youngest sister, Charlie, added.

"*Ja*, poor dear."

Peter frowned, disturbed that Meg was the topic of conversation. Why weren't her sisters inside keeping her company? He felt a sharp kick to his innards. Why hadn't he stayed awhile to talk with her?

But he knew the answer—because he needed to get over her. Which had been harder for him to do since the day he'd found her floating in the water after the accident.

The girls switched to another subject, and the pain in his stomach eased. He turned his attention elsewhere.

Directly across the table from him sat Eli and Jacob Lapp, with their wives, Martha and Annie. Annie held EJ in her lap, while Jacob had his arms filled with their daughter, Susanna. He studied them, glad his sister was happy with a man she loved and two beautiful children. He shifted his gaze from his little niece and found Annie eyeing him closely.

He arched his eyebrows. "What?"

His sister shrugged. "I guess you know what you're doing."

Peter stiffened. "What do you mean?"

"Not a *gut* time, *bruder*. Best if we talk later." Her impish look reminded him of all of the times during their childhood when she'd teased him.

"Annie…" Peter warned.

Jacob narrowed his gaze on Peter, then looked for an explanation from his wife. "Are you taunting Peter again?"

"With love, Jacob. Only with love," she murmured, her eyes soft as she regarded her husband, who tenderly shifted their young daughter on his lap, bringing her up to rest her sleepy head on his shoulder.

Peter felt restless. He turned to Agnes and touched her arm. "Want to go for a ride?"

Agnes faced him, her expression brightening. "We can if you'd like." She stood and pushed back her chair.

Peter hurried to help her. They were outside before she said, "I have an idea."

She headed toward the house, and he grinned with the thought of the desserts she'd pack for their buggy ride. But Agnes didn't head toward where the pies, cake and other goodies had been laid out. She went to Meg instead, seated in her wheelchair, finishing the last bite of her meal.

"Meg," Agnes said in greeting as he stood silently behind her. "We're going for a ride. Would you like to come?"

Meg appeared stunned by the invitation. Peter studied her, recognizing her surprise and confusion. She looked tired, as if the day had already been too much for her. The bruises on her face were more pronounced than they'd been when she was in the hospital. He should offer to drive her home, but he didn't think she'd appreciate it any more than she did Agnes's invitation. He'd known her long enough to read the subtle changes in her gaze that told him when she was overwhelmed and uncomfortable.

"*Danki*, Agnes," she said quietly. "It's kind of you to ask, but I'm not feeling my best, so it would be better if I just stayed here." Meg managed a smile. Peter couldn't help but feel relieved.

Agnes frowned. "I don't like seeing you sitting here alone."

Meg's expression made Peter ache. The last thing she wanted, he was sure, was for Agnes to try to change her mind while he watched. He touched Agnes's arm. "She's not feeling well, Agnes."

Agnes shot him a look. "I know." She turned a sympathetic gaze on Meg. "Rest now. I'm sorry I can't do anything to help."

"*Danki.*" Meg sounded suspiciously close to tears. Peter couldn't tear his eyes away from her. Despite her bruises, she looked beautiful. The royal blue dress she wore intensified the bright azure of her eyes. Her white prayer *kapp* was slightly askew, revealing shiny dark hair pulled back in the Amish way. Her gaze fell on him, and he had to glance away before he did something ridiculous like reach over, pick her up and carry her to his buggy to take her home.

Instead he followed Agnes from the room. Once outside, she faced him. "Let's not go for a ride. Why don't we go for a walk instead? I'll ask Alice to join us."

"The weather is nice enough," he agreed, as he followed her back toward the barn. Agnes went to talk with her sister. Unable to forget how tired Meg looked, Peter headed toward his sister Annie.

Meg was chatting with her mother and aunt when Jacob and Annie entered the kitchen from outside.

"Meg, we thought you might like to go home." Jacob smiled as he approached, carrying his daughter. "'Tis been a long day for you."

"We can take her," *Mam* immediately said.

"No need," Annie assured her. "Our little ones are ready to be home."

"Are you sure you don't mind?" Meg asked, delighted by Jacob's offer. She wanted nothing more than to rest.

"I don't think you should be alone," her mother murmured with concern.

"*Mam*, I'll be fine. I'll take a nap. Please stay here and enjoy yourself."

"We can stay with her for a while." Annie picked up EJ, who had been holding on to her hand.

Meg gazed at her cousin-in-law gratefully. "*Mam*, I'll be fine. I'm not seriously injured. I have a broken leg."

"I should check with your *vadder*."

"*Nay!*" Meg exclaimed. "You know how *Dat* is. He'll want to bring me home. He's enjoying himself, *Mam*. I'll be fine for a couple of hours. Honestly. I'll just close my eyes and sleep."

"*Endie* Missy, Meg will be fine," Jacob assured her. "I'll make certain of it."

Her mother stood and retrieved Meg's coat. "*Oll recht*. I'll see you at home a little later."

Feeling sore and highly emotional, Meg rolled her chair closer to her mother. "I love you," she whispered with tears of gratitude.

Soon, she was riding in Jacob and Annie's buggy, with EJ seated next to her and Susanna on her mother's lap up front. Jacob had stowed her wheelchair behind Meg's seat.

She was never so glad to see her home as when Jacob pulled into the barnyard and parked close to the house. She watched him take out her wheelchair first. She expected him to open it for her, but he placed it near the porch instead, then came back to carry her up the steps and on inside. "*Danki.*"

"You're *willkomm*," her cousin said with a grin. His good humor faded quickly, though. "I wish I'd thought to bring you home earlier. I should have suspected you weren't ready to be visiting."

Meg shook her head. "I didn't want *Dat* and *Mam* to stay home because of me. They would have refused to go if I'd admitted I wasn't feeling well."

"Poor Meg," Annie murmured with sympathy as she followed them into the great room.

Jacob placed Meg into a chair and went outside for her wheelchair.

"You look exhausted," Annie said as she sat on the sofa not far from where Meg was seated. "Would you be more comfortable here?"

"*Nay*, I like it here," Meg assured her. "I can look out the window."

Jacob entered the room and set the wheelchair near

the far wall. Meg smiled her thanks, then studied the children, who played on the floor near their mother. "I'll be *oll recht* by myself." She shifted her leg onto the stool her father recently had handmade for her. "I appreciate your help."

Annie smiled. "You gave us a *gut* excuse to get these little ones settled at home." She watched fondly as the two chatted quietly.

"EJ is a wonderful big *bruder*."

The boy's mother laughed. "Most of the time, but not always."

Her husband agreed. "He's a *gut* boy, though."

"He looks like Elijah," Meg said without thinking.

Jacob's short bark of laughter startled her. "That's what Eli says. Blond hair and blue eyes. But my *bruder* is not the only one with those features." He fondly eyed his wife.

Meg couldn't help the small smile that came to her lips. "*Ja*, he does look like his *mam*, but he looks like his *dat*, too."

Her cousin beamed at her.

"Now, go home!" Meg ordered.

Jacob blinked at her vehemence. "I told your *mam* we'd stay for a while."

"And you did. Now, take your little ones home."

"Can we get you anything before we go?" Annie asked, her gaze sharp.

"I've had too much to eat and more than enough to drink today. I'll be fine."

Jacob picked up his son while Annie reached for their daughter.

"Thanks for noticing how tired I am," Meg said.

Her cousin shook his head. "Don't thank us. The

credit goes to Peter. He's the one who suggested you might like to go home."

The young family left, leaving Meg with a lot to think about. It was as if Peter had read her mind again. The realization unsettled her.

Her parents and sisters came home an hour and a half later. Her father didn't look happy as he entered the great room.

"I'm well, *Dat*," she said, before he could speak. "Jacob and Annie made sure I was settled before they left."

"You should have told us you wanted to go." He looked upset. "I should have known it was too soon for you."

"I'm fine. Please don't worry about me."

Dat regarded her with what looked suspiciously like tears in his eyes.

"I could eat, though," she said teasingly, and she saw the worry leave his expression.

"Supper will be ready soon." He turned to leave.

"Dat." He faced her. *"Danki* for caring," she said.

His expression grew soft. "I'm your *vadder.*"

The evening passed quietly after a simple meal of cold cuts and fresh bread, followed by apple pie. Meg hadn't actually slept after Jacob had brought her home, but she had rested. It didn't take long for her to fall asleep once she'd retired for the night.

She woke up to the sounds of birds outside her window the next morning. She relished the pleasant sensation of lying in bed, listening to birdsong, until it hit her. Peter. Alarmed, she sat up. She was going to be working with Peter for weeks, planning their parents' party.

She closed her eyes, recalling the way he had studied her when she'd last seen him. He'd been kind to her recently, and he'd convinced Jacob to take her home. She didn't know what to make of his thoughtfulness.

She stood, grabbed her crutches and tried not to think of him. But his face remained ever present in her thoughts.

Chapter Five

Monday afternoon Peter paused at the base of the stairs and stared up at the Stoltzfus farmhouse. The last thing he'd expected to be working on was planning a birthday party for his mother and Arlin Stoltzfus. He had learned about Missy Stoltzfus's and his father's arrangement to have him and Meg work together to plan the celebration the evening of the last singing, the night that Reuben Miller and Meg had had the accident. Peter had figured that because of the accident, their parents would have forgotten all about the arrangement. But apparently not. So here he stood, in front of Meg's house, after being told by his father this morning that Missy and Meg would be expecting him today.

He thought about Meg. How on earth was he going to work with her? Meg Stoltzfus could be difficult on a good day. Planning an event with her wasn't going to be easy.

He grinned as he realized that he was up for the challenge.

He thought of Agnes and the wonderful afternoon they'd shared on their walk with Alice. The three of them had chatted, laughed and had a nice time. It had been a stress-free afternoon. Still, he had thought of Meg during it. It felt as though something was missing when he spent time with Agnes.

Peter climbed the steps and knocked.

Meg's mother opened the door. "Peter!" She smiled as she stepped back to allow him entry. "Come in. Meg is in the great room."

"Is she feeling *oll recht*?" he asked, as he followed her through the kitchen.

"She's coming along," Missy said.

As he entered the room, he caught sight of Meg immediately, seated in a chair facing the window. She looked pensive as she gazed out into the yard.

"Meg, Peter's here."

She jerked as if burned, and met his gaze. "*Hallo*, Peter." She lifted her cast off a stool and tried to turn her chair.

He rushed forward to help, gently grabbing the back of her chair and swiveling it to face the room. He then retrieved the large stool she'd been resting her leg on and placed it directly in front of her.

Meg gave him an irritated look as she lifted both legs onto the stool. Clearly, she wasn't happy to accept his help. If this was the way their planning time would go, then it was going to be much more challenging than he'd envisioned.

He grabbed a wooden chair from the other side of the room and sat, facing her. She seemed much improved since yesterday. "You look better. You must have slept well."

She stared at him, then arched an eyebrow. "Why are you so concerned about my sleeping habits, Peter?"

He stiffened, no longer feeling sorry for her. "Who says that I am?"

"I don't like to be treated like an invalid."

He snorted. "Have I treated you that way?"

Meg sighed, and he watched as her anger deflated. "I apologize. I'm frustrated and feeling sorry for myself. You don't deserve the way I spoke to you." She reached to brush back a tiny strand of hair that had escaped from beneath her prayer *kapp*. She wore a bright purple dress, which looked lovely with her dark hair and blue eyes. Peter couldn't help admiring her as she reached for the quilt on a nearby table. She covered her legs, then met his gaze. "So, we're going to plan a party together."

"Ja," he said. "You up for the challenge?"

Her eyes widened before she choked out a laugh. "Direct," she said. "I like that." She gazed at him, and he stared back until she looked away.

"Your *vadder* is not home?"

Meg shook her head. "He's with *Onkel* Samuel. He'll be gone all day." She paused. "My sisters, too."

"Where do you think we should start?"

"How about a place to have the party?"

"We can have it at our *haus,*" Peter suggested.

She wrinkled her nose. "Bad idea."

He frowned. "Why?"

"How will we keep it a surprise if it's at either of our houses? Your *mudder* and my *vadder* will figure out that something is going on." She fingered a bruise at her temple.

"Sore?" he asked, concerned despite himself.

She stiffened. "I'm fine."

"I didn't say you weren't, Meg," he said with patience. "I just wondered if that bruise is bothering you. I didn't mean to imply anything but concern."

"Sorry." Meg briefly closed her eyes. "Both," she admitted.

"Would you rather I come back another day?"

"Nay." She straightened her spine as if her pain had diminished, except he saw something in her eyes that said otherwise. "We need to get started on this. Christmas is next month. There isn't much time."

He inclined his head. "What about at your *endie* Katie's?" he suggested.

She shook her head. "Won't work. *Dat* is over there almost as much as he is here."

Peter stifled irritation. "Then where, Meg? Where would you like to have it?"

"I don't know!"

"Maybe we both should give it some thought," he said. "We'll need a location where neither one will suspect a party if our families decide to visit."

"Ja." Meg touched her prayer *kapp* as if wanting to straighten it. Her head covering looked fine to Peter, who wondered if something other than pain was causing her to shift uncomfortably in her seat. "I can't think of any place."

"Let's forget about a location for now," Peter suggested.

"But it's important!"

"Ja, I know, but we can put off talking about it until the next time we meet. *Oll recht?"*

"Ja."

Missy Stoltzfus entered the room and seemed pleased to see them working together. "Would either of you like anything to eat or drink?" she asked.

"I could use a cup of tea, *Mam.*"

Peter's lips curved. "I'll have the same."

Her mother grinned. "Coming up. Cookies?"

"Ja, that would be nice," he replied, as Meg said the

same thing. He met her glance, and he was startled but pleased when they shared a smile.

"What next?" Meg asked after a lengthy silence.

Peter gave it some thought. "Food? How about the cake? My *mudder* loves chocolate."

Meg frowned. "*Dat* prefers lemon."

"Another topic for our next meeting?" Peter suggested drily.

She glared at him. "We haven't agreed on anything."

"This is only the first time we've met, Meg. I'm sure we'll work it out." At least, he hoped so. He had the feeling she would disagree with all his suggestions just to be contrary.

"Here's your tea," Missy announced as she returned. She handed them each a steaming cup and set a plate of cookies on the table. "I put sugar and milk in it."

Meg smiled before she took a tentative sip. "That's *gut, Mam.*"

Peter took a drink. "*Ja,* delicious, Missy." He gave her a lopsided smile. Finally, there was something he and Meg agreed on.

They drank their tea and ate chocolate chip cookies silently. Peter studied his planning partner, saw her normally bright eyes dim. Clearly, she'd had enough party planning for one day.

"I should go."

She gazed at him but didn't disagree, which told him just how exhausted she was. Or how quickly she wanted to be rid of him. "Wednesday?" she asked.

"Will your *dat* be home?"

"*Mam!*" she called.

Missy appeared in the doorway. "*Ja, dochter?*"

"Will *Dat* be home on Wednesday? Peter and I want to meet again."

Amused by Meg's choice of words, Peter hid a smile.

Her mother frowned. "I don't think so. Samuel's project is supposed to take a couple of days. I'll let you know if that changes." She eyed them both carefully. "Good start in planning? I guess you had enough for today."

"*Ja*, Missy. I need to get home." And Meg needed something for her headache, he thought. "I'll see you on Wednesday, Meg."

"See you then, Peter."

Missy walked him to the door. Peter paused with his hand on the doorknob. "She has a headache."

Her mother understood. "I'll get her pain medication."

Satisfied, he left, feeling as though he could breathe again. As he drove home, he went over every moment of their first planning meeting, brief as it had been. It was going to be hard for them to agree on anything, he realized. And while he'd asked whether or not Arlin would be home, he'd never given any thought to Meg's sisters. His father, Horseshoe Joe, had insisted that the party be a secret best kept to themselves. If others found out about it, then the surprise for their parents could be ruined.

This was going to be more complicated than he'd originally thought.

After Peter left, Meg leaned her head back and closed her eyes. She had a doozy of a headache, and every muscle in her body seemed to ache.

"Meg." Her *mam* came into the room. She handed Meg a glass of water and a white pill. "Peter said you have a headache."

It frightened her how Peter could read her so well. "*Mam*, I'll be fine. I don't need this."

"*Ja*, you do. You've barely taken anything since you've been home. Take it, Meg, so that you can rest and recover."

Meg sighed before she swallowed the pill with the water.

"Would you like to lie down?" *Mam* asked.

"I guess so."

With her mother's help, Meg crossed to the sewing room and lay on the bed.

"Sleep well, *dochter*. I'll call you when 'tis time to eat."

"I love you, *Mam*."

The next morning, Meg was in the kitchen, helping Leah and Ellie bake bread. Charlie had gone with their mother to visit Nell. Leah and Ellie assembled the dough, then Ellie dumped hers onto a wooden cutting board dusted with flour. Meg pulled it close and began to knead awkwardly. It wasn't easy while sitting down, but she wasn't going to complain. This simple chore was the least she could do when her sisters and mother were handling the rest of the housework.

"How are you making out with that, Meg?" Leah said.

"*Gut.*" Meg's lips curved upward. "I haven't been much help. I'm glad to do this."

"Meg," Ellie said softly, "you were in a terrible accident. We don't expect you to work."

"I like to help. I don't like feeling as if I'm not contributing."

"Ellie's right, Meg." Leah regarded her with a concerned gaze. "You shouldn't overdo it." Suddenly, she grinned. "There will be plenty of time for you to make it up to us later."

Meg laughed. "I'm sure."

A loud knock sounded on the back door that led outside from the kitchen.

Ellie went to open it. "Why, *hallo*! 'Tis nice of you to stop by!" She turned to Meg. "There's someone here to see you."

Meg looked up into Reuben's blue eyes. Relief that it wasn't Peter hit her full force and she beamed at him. "Reuben! Come in!"

Leah pulled a chair for him close to the worktable next to Meg.

Reuben wore a dark jacket over a royal blue shirt, with dark blue tri-blend denim pants held up by black suspenders. He had taken off his black-banded straw hat and held it in his right hand. He turned and hung the hat on a wooden peg near the door before he approached Meg and sat down. "You're looking better, Meg," he said, beaming.

"You are, too. Any lingering problems?"

"*Nay*, you?" His gaze dropped down to her cast beneath the table. "How is your leg?"

"I can't stand on it, but it doesn't hurt as much as it did."

"I'm glad."

"Reuben," Ellie said, "would you like a cup of coffee? There's some on the stove."

"That would be wonderful, Ellie."

Meg noted with interest that her sister blushed as she turned to get his coffee. "Did you get Eli to take a look at your buggy?"

His expression sobering, he nodded. "Hopeless, I'm afraid. I've commissioned him to make me a new one."

She blinked, surprised that he had the money for a new carriage.

"Your cousin has taken the old one for parts. He's giving me credit for them."

That was something Eli would do, she thought with affection.

"Since you're here, I'm guessing you're not back to work yet." Meg stated.

"Actually, I am, but I don't have to go until this afternoon."

"I see."

As they talked, she continued to knead the bread dough. Suddenly, he reached out to still her hands. At his touch, she froze and shot her sisters a glance. They were too busy washing bowls and utensils to notice.

"Meg."

Her breath stilled. *"Ja?"*

"I hope you've forgiven me," he said, too softly for her sisters to hear.

She eyed him with confusion. "For what?"

"The accident."

"Reuben, the accident wasn't your fault. There is nothing to forgive."

"Then you'll spend time with me again? Go for another ride after I get my new buggy?"

She nodded.

He appeared pleased. *"Gut.* I care about you, Meg." His mouth curved. "A lot."

The man had saved her life, she reminded herself. "You're a *gut* man, Reuben Miller," she said warmly.

"Here's your coffee," Ellie said, placing a cup in front of him. "I heated it up. If it's too strong, I'll make a fresh pot."

Reuben sipped from the cup. "'Tis *gut*, Ellie."

Her sister beamed. There was another rap on the back door just then and she went to answer it.

"Peter! Agnes! Nice to see you!"

"We've come to see how Meg's faring," Agnes said.

"Come in," Leah invited from across the room. "It seems to be a day for visitors."

Meg was startled by the couple's visit. She saw Agnes first. The girl's gaze brightened as it homed in on her. "Meg!" She hurried forward. "Oh, *hallo*, Reuben."

"*Hallo*, Agnes." Meg rolled the prepared bread dough and handed it to Ellie, who set it in the oven.

Reuben's expression was pleasant as he returned Agnes's greeting, but his features darkened when he looked at her companion. "Peter," he said.

"Reuben." Peter returned the greeting quietly. He met Meg's gaze. "Feeling better?"

"*Ja*, I'm doing well."

With an amused smile, he nodded before he approached her sisters. As she watched him speak with Leah and Ellie, Meg couldn't help but notice how good Peter looked in his black jacket with a green shirt and tri-blend pants. There was no sign of his hat, so she figured he'd left it in his vehicle or at home.

"It will be a fun outing," Agnes said, drawing Meg's attention. She realized that Agnes was talking with Reuben. "The four of us can go to lunch and then for a ride. That would be fun, *ja*?"

"*Ja*," Reuben agreed. "Meg? Are you up for lunch and a ride with Agnes and Peter one day this week?"

"I...I guess so." She glanced briefly at Peter. He looked about as enthused as she felt. "When?" She didn't want to go, but didn't wish to be rude, either, and Reuben appeared excited by the prospect. She wanted to make him happy because of everything he'd done for her.

"How about tomorrow at eleven?" Agnes suggested. "Reuben, will you be able to get off from work?"

"*Ja*. The crew is finishing up a job today. I should be free." His gaze warmed as it settled on Meg. "Meg?"

"I'm not busy these days." Her eyes widened a bit as she met Peter's gaze. They were supposed to meet again tomorrow. They couldn't on Thursday, since it was Thanksgiving. She caught his barely perceptible nod. "I don't think I have anything to do, but I'll need to make sure I don't have a doctor's appointment."

"*Wunderbor!*" Agnes exclaimed, as if the arrangements were settled. "We'll have a great time." She turned to Peter. "Won't we?"

"Great time," he echoed, but Meg could tell that he wasn't particularly excited.

Shortly afterward, Peter and Agnes got up to leave. While Agnes and Reuben chatted, Peter mouthed to Meg, "Eight?" Then she understood and dipped her head in agreement. He would come at eight for their meeting before he picked up Agnes later that morning.

"Lunch and a drive sounds like fun," Reuben said, when the others had left.

"*Ja*. Did you decide on a place to eat?"

He frowned, then his brow cleared as he laughed. "We didn't talk about that. I'm sure Agnes has something in mind."

Meg inclined her head. "I'm sure she does."

Reuben glanced at his watch, then stood. "I've got to go, Meg. You'll be fine here."

"I'm at home, Reuben," she teased. "Why wouldn't I be?"

He went to the door and reached for his hat. "I'll see you tomorrow at ten thirty."

Was she destined to see Peter every day? Meg wondered, after Reuben had left. She closed her eyes. It was bad enough she and Peter had to work together. The last thing she needed on top of that was for her and Reuben to be spending leisure time with him and Agnes.

Chapter Six

"I thought we could go to Honeysuckle and eat lunch at Margaret's Restaurant. Do you know it? Then afterward we can go for a drive before we take Meg and Reuben back to Meg's."

Peter listened to Agnes talk about the planned outing and felt his stomach burn. He didn't want to go anywhere with the other couple. It was bad enough that he had to spend time with Meg to plan the birthday party. The last thing he wanted to do was to go out socially with her and her new sweetheart.

"Honeysuckle is awfully far. We'd have to leave early in the morning, and we said we'd go at eleven. Besides, I'm not sure Meg is up to it yet. In fact, I'm not sure she is up for an outing at all. She's only been out of the hospital a week."

"*Ja*, but she's excited to go—and so is Reuben. Did you see the way his eyes lit up? Maybe Honeysuckle *is* too far. Where do you think we should go?"

He hadn't seen Meg's excitement. He'd glimpsed only wariness in her eyes until she'd recognized Reuben's delight. Then she'd relented and seemed willing to go. "I don't know, Agnes. I still have reservations."

Her silence told him that she wasn't happy with him. "Why? Is it Meg? You don't want to spend time with her? Or is it that you don't like seeing Meg with Reuben? Think about it, Peter. We can have fun. We won't go far. You have a point about Honeysuckle being a long drive, especially since you'll be the one taking us... You don't mind if we go in your buggy, do you?"

He turned to her. "I don't mind driving," he assured her with a smile. How could he not catch a glimmer of her infectious excitement?

She beamed at him. "We'll have a *gut* time. You'll see."

Peter continued to listen as he steered his horse and buggy down the road toward the Joshua Beiler home.

"What about the diner in Ephrata?" Agnes suggested.

"That would take about an hour and a half to get there. We're supposed to go for a drive afterward, *ja*?" He glanced over to see her nod. "Then we should go someplace closer."

"How about the Family Restaurant in New Holland?"

"I don't have a problem with that. It takes half the time to get to New Holland as it does to Ephrata."

"*Wunderbor!* Then it's all settled." She touched his arm. "*Danki*, Peter. I'm looking forward to this!"

Peter managed to grin at her, even though, despite her excitement, he was not looking forward to tomorrow's trip. But he wanted things to work between him and Agnes. He liked her. She'd been a good friend for almost a year. He would do this simply because it made her happy. Besides, he had to learn to accept the fact that Meg was with Reuben now and he would be seeing them together frequently.

He dropped Agnes at her house with the promise of picking her up at ten forty-five the next day, then headed home. He pulled onto the dirt lane that took him past Annie and Jacob's house on the left, then toward the main farmhouse, with his father's blacksmith shop in the barn next to it. He parked, took care of his horse, then on impulse headed toward Zook's Blacksmithy, hoping to get a private word with Jacob, who worked there. His brother-in-law was Horseshoe Joe's partner in the business.

He was in luck. Jacob was alone. His father had gone into the house, probably to eat his midday meal. Jacob had the fire in the furnace going, and Peter watched as he pulled a bright red piece of metal from the flame, then bent it into a horseshoe by striking it with a hammer on the heavy iron anvil.

Peter waited patiently as Jacob held the metal up to inspect it, before hammering it some more. He needed to talk with his brother-in-law, but didn't want to scare him. Because of his carelessness, he'd once gotten Jacob burned when he'd startled him while he was working with hot metal. He was more careful now. He had no intention of doing that again.

Jacob stopped hammering, held up the horseshoe once more, and then, apparently satisfied, set the bright glowing metal onto the anvil to cool. He stepped back, and Peter knew he was done.

"Jake?"

His brother-in-law turned to him with surprised delight in his brown gaze. "Peter! Come in."

"I didn't want to scare you."

"You didn't." Jacob removed his gloves and set them on a table under several wall shelves. "If you're looking for your *dat*, he's not here."

"*Nay.* I came to see you."

"I'm heading down to the house for lunch. Come with me. Your sister will be happy to see you."

Peter hesitated. "You know she'll be nosy, *ja*?"

Jacob laughed. "She's your *schweschter*. *Ja*, she'll be nosy."

They left the barn and started down the lane toward the small house that had been built about a hundred feet off the main road.

"Your sister loves you, Peter. She wouldn't intentionally hurt you."

He sighed. "*Ja*, I know. But I saw the way she looked at me and Agnes together the other day, and it's clear she has something she wants to say to me." He paused. "I'm not sure I want to hear it."

"Peter, are you afraid of my wife?"

"Sure am."

Jacob chuckled. "I don't think it's Annie you wanted to discuss with me. What is it?"

"Agnes," Peter said. "And Meg."

"Ah, the two women in your life."

"Meg isn't in my life."

His brother-in-law arched an eyebrow. "But Agnes is."

"They *are* both in my life, but not in the same way. Meg… She's with Reuben now. I've decided to move on. Agnes has been a *gut* friend for a long time. I like her. Why shouldn't we be more than friends?"

"No reason why you can't be more," Jacob reasoned. "But is that what you really want? To forget about Meg and move on with Agnes?"

"I think it's a wise thing to do."

Her sister's husband nodded. "Then that's *gut*." He was quiet a moment. "Agnes is a nice girl."

"*Ja*, she is." But then he always felt that Meg could be a nice girl, too, if she wanted to be.

The gravel on the road crunched beneath their feet.

"I really cared for your cousin," Peter admitted after a lengthy silence.

"I know." Jacob eyed him with sympathy. "Women aren't easy to understand."

"How did you win Annie's heart?" He glanced toward the man, who he respected and admired.

"You want to know this to win Meg's? Or improve things with Agnes?"

"Agnes," he said quickly. Too quickly. It was just so difficult to forget about Meg when he'd liked her for so long. "You must know the secret to courting a woman. You managed to get my sister."

"And you think I simply courted her and she fell in love with me?" Jacob asked with disbelief. "Peter, I've loved your sister since I was eleven. She never looked twice at me, and even when she finally did, she refused to have anything to do with me. She was still suffering a broken heart from her previous relationship with my *bruder* Jed. And that only complicated matters. I nearly gave up on her. I don't know when it happened, but suddenly she was there, telling me she loved me. I almost didn't believe it. When it finally sunk in, I was the happiest man alive." His smile lit up his eyes. "I still am."

"I want that. I want what you and Annie have."

"Then be persistent, until you can't do any more. If the Lord wants you and Agnes to be together, then you will be."

Agnes, Peter thought. They were talking about Agnes, but silently he was thinking of Meg, who was with someone else, but still owned a huge piece of his heart.

They reached the cottage, and Jacob went in through the back door, Peter following closely behind.

"Annie, I'm home!" Jacob called, when there was no sign of his wife in the kitchen.

"I'll be right there!"

"I've brought company for lunch."

"Who?" Annie asked, as she emerged, carrying her daughter on her hip and holding her son's hand.

"Peter." Jacob hurried to relieve her burden, pulling their daughter into his arms.

Annie's gaze speared her brother from across the room. "Peter's not company. He's family." Her expression was warm. "*Hallo, bruder.* Are you hungry?"

"I could eat." Peter was glad to see her, although he knew he'd change his mind within minutes if she started to grill him about his relationships with Agnes and Meg.

"Are your hands clean?" she asked.

Peter went to the kitchen sink and washed. He turned and showed her his palms. "They are now, *Mam.*" He grinned.

Annie laughed. "Sit down and I'll serve lunch. Jacob, would you please pull out a chair for EJ?"

"*Ja.*" He put EJ in a chair, then sat with Susanna on his lap, and the little girl appeared perfectly content.

Soon, they were all seated and eating lunch. The food was good. Annie had made Amish chicken potpie made with tasty, thick noodles, and the delicious aroma of the dish wafted through the kitchen, causing Peter's stomach to growl. When they were done eating, he thanked his sister and Jacob, excused himself as he rose from the table.

"So what's this I hear about you seeing Agnes?" Annie asked in her usual frank manner as he pushed in his chair.

Peter shifted uncomfortably. "She's a friend. You know that."

"Just a friend?" His sister raised an eyebrow. "And Meg?"

He glanced away. "Meg is Meg," he muttered.

Annie was silent a long moment. "Are you *oll recht*?"

He looked at her, surprised to see compassion in her blue eyes. *"Ja,"* he said.

"You know you can talk to me, and I won't judge." She gave him a crooked smile. "I may tease at times but not when something's bothering you." Her voice softened. "Not when 'tis important."

He swallowed against a sudden lump as he nodded.

"Go on!" she said. "Get out of here. I know you're eager to get away."

After a quick glance in Jacob's direction, he grabbed his hat on his way to the door. He halted and faced his sister. *"Danki,* Annie."

Early the next morning, Meg sat with her cast propped up on the chair on the other side of the kitchen table as she waited for Peter. She had a pencil and paper to take notes regarding decisions about the birthday party. Since their first meeting, she'd thought long and hard about a place for the party. It had come to her, as thoughts sometimes did, during the night. Bishop John Fisher's house would be an ideal location. He was a widower with one small son and a house large enough for a good-sized crowd. That was, if they could convince him to host it. The bishop's wife had died this past summer, and the loss had been hard on him.

Meg wondered if Peter had come up with an idea for a location. She doubted he'd thought of one better than Bishop John's. Would he agree with her suggestion or give her a hard time? Sometimes she thought he was being difficult just to annoy her. She hoped she was wrong, but it certainly seemed that way.

The house was quiet. Her mother had found an excuse to send her father and sisters out of there early. The only one home was *Mam*, who'd said she would be busy upstairs all morning doing chores. Meg still felt bad that she couldn't be of more help in the house, but when she'd mentioned it, her mother had quickly waved away her concerns. "You're planning the party for me, Meg," she'd said. "It's a huge chore, and one I'm happy to leave in your and Peter's capable hands."

At precisely eight o'clock, she heard a knock on the back door. Meg felt a fluttering in her belly. Peter had arrived. She didn't get up. She was afraid she'd be clumsy and fall if she tried. "Come in!" she called loudly.

The doorknob turned before the door swung open and Peter stepped inside. The man looked way too handsome for her peace of mind in a blue tri-blend jacket and matching pants.

"Morning, Meg." He took off his hat and set it on the end of the table.

"*Hallo*, Peter," she said. She watched as he removed his coat. Meg's gaze went to his maroon shirt, which fit him well. The contrast in color emphasized the dark gray of his eyes.

"Ready to get started?" He skirted the table and pulled out the chair next to her. He hung his coat on its back before he sat down. "We don't have much time."

"*Ja.*" She knew he referred to their eleven o'clock outing with Agnes and Reuben, but she didn't want to get into a discussion about it, in case it set a bad tone for their working together. "Everyone is gone but *Mam*, and she'll be busy upstairs for a while." She tried to act casual with him so near.

"What's that?" He shifted closer and gestured toward the paper before her.

Meg felt her neck tingle. He smelled like soap, outdoors and something uniquely Peter. She'd never been so aware of him as a man. "I thought I'd make note of our ideas and keep a record of our decisions."

"*Gut* idea." He glanced up, and she felt a jolt from the impact of his gray eyes. "What shall we discuss first? The location? I have an idea that you may like."

"I bet I have a better place," she challenged.

"And where is this *better* place?" he asked with a little smirk. "You haven't heard mine yet."

"Bishop John Fisher's *haus*."

Peter laughed.

"What's so funny?" she asked, offended.

He sobered instantly. "We came up with the same idea."

Meg blinked. "Honestly?"

"*Ja*. I know he just lost his wife, but he has a large enough house, and I was thinking that at Christmas he might be feeling lonely. If we have the party there, he'll be surrounded by family and friends, and it might make the holidays more bearable for him."

"My thoughts exactly," she said.

They looked at each other and grinned.

"Looks like we've found something we both actually agree on!" Meg was pleased. It seemed that this meeting would go smoother than the first one. "It may take some convincing."

Peter sighed. "*Ja*, that could prove difficult. We should pay him a visit." He appeared to give it some thought. "Can't tomorrow."

Meg nodded. Tomorrow was Thanksgiving. "Friday?"

"I'm free," he said.

"Would you mind bringing me?"

"Not at all. We should go together. We're planning partners, after all."

Meg hid a smile. She liked that he'd acknowledged they were in this together. Filled with good humor, she wrote down Bishop John's name followed by a question mark. When Peter raised his eyebrows, she said, "Until we can get him to agree."

"Makes sense." Peter stared at her list. "What next? The cake?"

"My *dat* still prefers lemon."

"And my *mudder* still loves chocolate." He thought for a moment. "Maybe a lemon cake with chocolate frosting?"

"*Ach, nay,* that sounds awful!"

Peter shrugged. "I suppose we could have two cakes, one for your *vadder* and another for my *mudder.*"

"We'll need to know how many guests are coming first," Meg said. "If it turns out to be a small party, we certainly won't need two cakes."

"We could always order a half lemon, half chocolate cake from Maggie Mast's bakery."

Meg stared at him. "That could work." She scribbled *cake with two halves* under *Bishop John* on her paper.

"What else do we need to discuss?"

"The invitation list," Meg said, then wrote that down.

"Food other than cake," Peter added.

Meg scribbled on. "Travel in the event of snow."

"*Gut* one!" Peter applauded, and Meg blushed, unused to his praise.

She felt strangely happy. She and Peter were getting along and coming up with ideas. The meeting so far had been a productive one. She was optimistic that the two of them could pull this off in a way that would surprise and please their parents.

"Would you like something to eat and drink?" Meg asked, relaxing now that things were going so well.

"*Nay*, but thanks." He shifted away from her, and Meg was stunned how the simple movement caused a chill in the room, where before there had been only warmth. "I was thinking we should wait until we visit Bishop John and get him to agree before we do anything else. What do you think?"

"That's probably the best idea," she agreed.

"What time on Friday?"

"Nine? Or is that too early?"

He shot her an annoyed look. "I came at eight this morning," he reminded her. "Do you actually think that I usually sleep past nine?"

"You don't?" she said, straight-faced.

"*Nay.*" He narrowed his eyes as if debating whether or not she was teasing. Then he smiled. "Funny, Meg."

She laughed. Then a tender look entered his eyes that made her stop and catch her breath as he studied her. He was silent a long moment. Then he blinked, and his expression changed, his gaze becoming unreadable.

They talked for another half hour, trying to come up with any details they might have missed. Christmas decorations, for one.

Just before ten o'clock, Peter abruptly rose and grabbed his coat from the back of his chair. "I need to go. I have to pick up Agnes at ten forty-five."

Meg watched as he put a powerful arm into each sleeve. He pulled the edges of his coat closed and buttoned it before picking up his hat.

"We made a *gut* start today," he said softly.

"*Ja*, we did," she agreed.

He didn't move. "I'll see you in about an hour. Agnes and I will come for you and Reuben at eleven."

"Reuben said he'd be here by ten thirty."

"See you then," she heard him say, as put his hand on the doorknob. Then he left without looking back.

Chapter Seven

Reuben and Meg exited the Arlin Stoltzfus house and stepped onto the front porch as Peter pulled in to park his buggy close to the residence. His eyes focused on Meg, on crutches, as Reuben held the door open for her.

"Look! There they are!" Agnes exclaimed happily.

Peter tore his gaze from the couple to grin at the young woman beside him. She was a pretty girl, with blond hair and light blue eyes, which were focused on him. Her light blue dress with a white cape and apron emphasized the color of her eyes. "You're really excited about going today, aren't you?"

Agnes flashed him a smile. "*Ja!* We'll have a great time!" She opened her door and quickly climbed out of the vehicle. "I think they need help."

Exiting his side of the buggy slowly, Peter skirted the carriage, his jaw clenching as Reuben picked up Meg in his arms and carried her down the steps after handing her crutches to Agnes.

Meg laughed while she protested being carried. "Reuben! I can manage!"

"I don't want to take chances with you, Meg. Why struggle with crutches when I can make the stairs a little easier for you?" He bent close and whispered, "You mean a lot to me. Let me help you."

Peter heard. His chest tightened as Meg rewarded Reuben with a wide smile. The other man eyed the buggy, and Peter saw his intention to lift Meg into the back seat. He fought the urge to rush to help, and stayed where he was—for a few seconds. Then he moved closer, ready to offer assistance if needed.

Reuben lifted Meg into the vehicle without incident, then went around to get in on the side. Peter followed, and as he waited to enter last, Reuben scowled at him.

After Reuben climbed in next to Meg, Peter got in and picked up the leathers. Agnes slid in next to him, and he steered the buggy toward the main road.

"Where are we going?" Meg asked, after they'd been riding for several minutes.

Agnes turned in her seat to face her. "I thought we'd eat lunch in New Holland and then enjoy a drive before we head back."

"That sounds good, Agnes," Reuben said warmly. "Family Restaurant?"

"*Ja*, the food is delicious there."

He nodded in agreement. "With a wide variety of things to eat." He smiled. "I've been there a time or two."

Peter remained silent, all too aware of Agnes beside him, and Meg, with her sweetheart, in the back. He felt tense and anxious until the others began to talk about their families and their plans for Thanksgiving the next day. Then he found himself relaxing as he listened to the pleasant conversation. He thought of Meg and their outing to see Bishop John on Friday.

"Peter?"

He jolted. *"Ja?"*

"You've been quiet," Agnes said.

"Just enjoying the ride."

"Oh, we're here!" she exclaimed. "See? Pull in over there." She gestured toward the restaurant parking lot. "There should be a hitching post around back."

Peter parked the buggy and tied up his horse. Reuben climbed out next, then reached inside to help Meg. As he turned, Peter watched Meg rise and try to maneuver on one foot. Her cast was bulky, and she had trouble moving toward the door. Reuben got back inside, gently clasped her arm and tried to extract her from the carriage. Peter hurried around the buggy and waited to see if he could assist them. Agnes had gotten out and was watching.

"Reuben," Peter began quietly, "let me help."

The other man shot him an angry look. Taken aback by his hostility, Peter raised his hands and backed off, then watched in silence. He became upset when Meg winced several times while Reuben attempted to help her. He kept bumping her cast against the back of the front seat each time he tried. Meg didn't say a word, but Peter could tell she was hurting. Finally, she was out of the vehicle. He met her gaze, and she looked away, as if embarrassed.

Peter tried to catch Reuben's attention to silently convey his dismay over his unwillingness to accept help, but the man refused to meet his gaze, choosing to focus on Meg instead.

"You *oll recht*?" Reuben asked softly as he handed Meg her crutches.

"Ja." She managed a smile, but Peter could see the pain in her expression. He'd known Meg a lot longer than Reuben had, and knew how to read her.

"I'm sorry, Meg," Reuben murmured.

Her smile widened, becoming more genuine. "'Tis fine, Reuben. Let's go. I don't know about you, but I'm hungry."

Reuben grinned. "Me, too."

Peter was silent as they entered the building. He sensed Agnes's regard and flashed her a smile. "The place looks nice."

Agnes was slow to smile back. "The food is *gut*." She reached out to touch his arm as he turned away. "Peter."

He gazed at her silently.

"I'm sorry. I didn't think."

Peter frowned.

"She isn't ready to come out with us."

He released a sigh. "She could have said *nay*, Agnes," he told her softly, for her ears alone. "'Tis *oll recht*." But he wasn't about to allow Reuben to be stubborn and hurt Meg again. He had an idea of how things would go on the way home—whether Reuben liked it or not.

Soon, they were seated in the restaurant. Peter sat next to Agnes. Meg and Reuben on the opposite side of the table, with Peter directly across from Meg.

"What do you recommend?" Peter asked pleasantly. It was time to make the best of things.

"Their sandwiches are tasty," Agnes replied.

"Everything looks *gut*." He perused the menu and made his choice. The couples gave their orders to the waitress, then sat back to wait for their meals.

"It turned out to be a nice day," Meg said, as the server brought their drinks.

"*Ja*, we couldn't have asked for better November weather," Peter agreed. He ignored Reuben's narrowed gaze and reached for the lemonade he'd ordered.

* * *

Meg felt self-conscious after the fiasco of Reuben assisting her from the buggy. She didn't understand the tension between him and Peter. She'd felt it as Peter had waited while Reuben struggled to help her. The strained air between the two men had remained as they'd entered the restaurant. It had seemed to ease, finally, after they'd given their food orders. Then they'd sat back with drinks and struck up a conversation.

Meg was conscious of Reuben beside her and Peter across from her. Agnes was animated as she actively tried to keep the conversation going. Eyeing the young woman, Meg couldn't help but like Agnes Beiler. She was thoughtful and kind, as proved when she'd asked after Meg's well-being on visiting Sunday, and later when she and Peter had stopped in to see her. Meg understood what Peter saw in her.

As she listened and occasionally added to the conversation about the holiday weekend, she became aware of the other restaurant patrons staring at her. Meg touched her face. Did she look that bad? Her bruises weren't as sore as they'd been right after the accident, and she'd nearly forgotten about them.

She sighed. She should have stayed home. She didn't like being the object of scrutiny, no matter how well intended. She stared down at her hands, suddenly feeling out of place.

"Meg."

She looked up and straight into Peter's gray eyes. "Headache?" he inquired gently.

She shook her head. "I'm fine."

"Of course you are," Reuben assured her with warmth.

Peter arched an eyebrow, as if he didn't believe her. She held his gaze, determined to prove that she was well.

"So my *eldre* decided we'd invite my cousins to Thanksgiving," Agnes was saying. "They live in New Wilmington. *Mam* sent a letter inviting them two weeks ago."

"How long has it been since you've seen them?" Meg asked, curious. She avoided looking at Peter, but sensed his regard.

"Over a year. It will be fun to see them again." She paused to eat a potato chip. "They should arrive sometime this evening."

Meg smiled. "It was wonderful when we moved to Happiness. It had been too long since we'd seen our Lapp cousins. I know my *dat* missed *Endie* Katie."

"So you don't mind living here," Peter said, drawing her attention.

She shook her head. "*Nay.* I like where we live. I enjoy our church community."

"And that's all you enjoy?" Reuben teased.

Meg grinned. "Maybe not all," she admitted. She felt Peter stiffen, but when she glanced at him, he seemed relaxed.

The waitress brought their food, and soon they were enjoying their meal. Reuben's attention made her feel special. He was a handsome man with a gentle and teasing nature. *Just the type of man I need in my life*, she told herself.

They finished their lunch with dessert. Meg glanced at the chocolate cake that the server set before Peter, then eyed the lemon dessert she'd ordered. Her lips twitched as she recalled their disagreement about the birthday cake flavor.

To her surprise, he was watching her, his masculine mouth curved upward. They shared a moment, until Reuben drew her attention with a touch on her arm.

"How's your pudding?" he inquired pleasantly.

"*Gut.* 'Tis been a long time since I've enjoyed lemon pudding." She paused. "'Tis my *dat's* favorite flavor." She heard a snort from across the table, but when she glanced over, Peter was smiling at Agnes as they discussed her dessert—rice pudding topped with cinnamon.

When it was time to leave, Reuben picked up Meg's crutches and held them for her as she pushed back from the table. She rose on her good foot, and he clasped her upper arm until she was balanced evenly on the crutches. "*Danki*, Reuben," she murmured, conscious of Peter and Agnes waiting patiently behind them.

As Meg drew close to the exit, Reuben rushed to open the door. She beamed at him as she hobbled past without mishap. Fortunately, there were no steps to the building. He stood close, ready to catch her if she fell, but she found her way to the buggy without incident.

She paused when she reached the vehicle. The thought of hurting her leg as she climbed into the back seat didn't sit well with her. She waited patiently as she contemplated what to do. She wished she could be up front with Peter, but Agnes was his sweetheart and had the right to sit next to him.

Reuben took her crutches and rested them against the buggy. When he spanned her waist with his hands, Meg blushed, embarrassed and overly self-conscious at the touch she was unaccustomed to. "Let me help," he murmured as he started to lift her.

Her leg struck the buggy's edge, and she winced. She heard Reuben's quick apology as he set her down. He picked her up again a moment later, and nearly had her in when the cast bumped against the vehicle again.

"*Nay.*" Peter was suddenly close. "Reuben, Meg

needs to sit up front. She'll be more comfortable there."
He addressed Agnes softly. "Do you mind?"

"Of course not," she assured him.

Reuben looked as if he wanted to argue, but seemed
to think better of it. He touched Meg's shoulder. "Is that
oll recht, Meg?"

She nodded, relieved, and Reuben followed her
around the vehicle until he realized that he couldn't
help her, because he had to get into the back first. He
glared at Peter, sighed, then climbed aboard.

Peter waited patiently, then held out his hand. Meg
felt a fluttering in her belly as his warm fingers gripped
hers firmly. He placed his other hand at the side of her
waist. Without effort, he lifted her as if she weighed no
more than a feather. She didn't bump her leg, and it took
only seconds for him to get her settled on the front seat
before he went around to climb in beside her.

Agnes was chatting with Reuben. Peter glanced
at her as if to ensure that she was comfortable. After
what seemed an eternity, he picked up the leathers and
steered the buggy out of the parking lot and onto the
main road. Meg was grateful to be in the front seat.
Peter had understood what she needed and taken care
of it for her. She felt something soften inside her.

The countryside was beautiful. Although she'd lived
in Lancaster County for over four years, Meg still appreciated her surroundings. The farm fields had been
harvested, but the sight of them still gave her a little thrill. She loved how the land looked when it was
freshly tilled and seeded, then as the plants sprouted and
grew tall. Spending so much time in the hospital when
she'd been ill at fourteen had given her a healthy ap-
preciation for everything that was alive outdoors. Peter
remained silent, taking in the view, as well.

"Meg," Agnes said, "I'm sorry. I shouldn't have pushed for you to come."

"I'm fine," she answered. "I've enjoyed myself." And she realized that she had. Despite the bruises and dealing with her cast, she'd found the day more than pleasant.

She sensed Peter's look and met his gaze briefly. He appeared to be deciding whether or not she was telling the truth. Then something eased in his features.

"Look!" Agnes said. "There's a fox!"

"Where?" Meg glanced out the window, but saw nothing.

"In the field over there!"

"I see it," Reuben said, but Meg didn't.

"There, Meg." Peter gestured past her to an open field just ahead. "See?"

His voice was soft. She could detect the clean, masculine, pleasing scent of him. She swallowed hard. "*Ja*, I see it." She smiled and sent him a silent thank-you with her gaze.

Peter steered the buggy on a leisurely tour of the countryside before turning to head for home. Meg was exhausted by the time he drove onto the lane to her family farmhouse. He pulled close to the porch, got out and came around to help her.

But Reuben jumped out of the vehicle and rushed around the carriage, so he could reach her first. "*Danki*, Peter," he said pleasantly, "I'll help her."

Peter stepped back. Agnes climbed out and stood beside him. "It was fun," she said. "Let's do it again sometime."

Meg looked from Peter to Reuben. She couldn't read Peter's expression, but Reuben looked happy at the prospect of another outing. "It was a nice afternoon," Reuben said.

"I'm glad you had fun." Agnes shifted closer to Peter. "Rest well, Meg," she said, before she climbed back into his buggy.

"Peter," Meg murmured. "I'll see you Sunday."

Something flickered in his gray eyes. "*Ja*, Meg. Have a *gut* night." He turned toward Reuben. "You, too, Reuben." He extended his hand. The man hesitated before he finally shook it.

Meg stood by Reuben as Peter and Agnes left. "I'll be heading home. I know you must be tired." Reuben paused, and warmth entered his expression. "I'm glad we got to spend time together today."

She managed a smile. "*Ja*. Lunch was *gut*." She wrinkled her nose impishly. "The company wasn't bad, either."

"I'm sorry about your leg." He paused. "And that you had to sit up front."

Meg frowned. "It was fine, Reuben. This cast is bulky. It was easier to sit there."

"I'd have liked it if you were next to me in the back."

His words made her uncomfortable, but she let them go. "I should get inside."

"Will you be up for the next youth singing?" he asked.

"I won't know how I'll be feeling until closer to the time."

He opened his mouth as if to say something else, but then shut it. He reached for her hand and gave it a squeeze instead. "Enjoy your evening, Meg Stoltzfus."

"You, too, Reuben."

He insisted on carrying her up to the front porch before he left. She stood at the railing and waved to him as he drove away—and then her thoughts turned toward Peter and the outing to see Bishop John Fisher in two days. She wondered if Peter would comment on today's outing, or mention any of the awkwardness.

She turned and, using her crutches, went inside the house.

Chapter Eight

"Are you ready to go?" Peter asked.

Meg gasped and looked up. "I didn't know you were here."

Her mother entered the great room from behind him. "I told him to come right in." She eyed the two of them. "What are your plans for today?"

"We've figured out a location for the party." Meg explained about their idea to hold the celebration at Bishop John's.

Mam's gaze flickered. "'Tis a *gut* idea if you can convince him. He's had a tough time since Catherine passed."

"*Ja*, I know," Meg said.

"We thought it might be *gut* for him to have company at Christmas," Peter added. "To be surrounded by our community and people who care about him."

"That's true." Her mother looked thoughtful. "How long will you be gone?"

"Not long, I imagine." Peter approached Meg and reached for her crutches. "Is anyone expected back soon?"

"*Nay*, Arlin and my *dechter* are gone for the morning. If you're back by noon, you should be fine." *Mam* watched as Peter extended a hand to help Meg rise. "Since you're going to see John anyway, would you bring him a cake I baked for him this morning? I was going to ask Leah to drop it off after she got home, but you can do it instead."

Peter grinned. "I've got bread for him in the buggy from *Mam*. She baked extra before Thanksgiving."

"Everyone wants to help," Meg said, as her mother left to get the cake. Peter had released her hand, but she still felt the tingling of his touch on her fingers. "Do you think we'll be able to convince him?"

He handed her the crutches, and she slipped one under each arm. "*Ja*. It may be hard at first, but I think he'll agree in the end. It must be lonely for him in that house with just his son for company."

Mam entered the room with the cake. "We feel terrible about what John's going through." She watched approvingly as Meg maneuvered toward the door with her crutches. "Remember, your *vadder* will be back by noon."

"We'll be back before then," Peter assured her as he held the door open, first for *Mam* to precede them, then for Meg to hobble through. "I've got to work in the shop today. *Dat* and Jacob received some last-minute orders. With winter coming, everyone wants to make sure they're ready."

"We could have postponed the visit," Meg said with a frown. She felt bad for taking him from his work.

Peter flashed her a smile that made her heart race. "Why? You think I'd rather be working in the shop? *Dat* doesn't need me until later. I think we should get the place for the party settled before doing anything else."

Meg nodded. That was what they'd discussed, and it made good sense.

"I'll have lunch ready for when you return," *Mam* promised as she reached the bottom of the steps. She headed toward the buggy with the cake.

"That's kind of you, Missy." Peter didn't rush to carry Meg as Reuben had, but waited patiently for her to manage the porch stairs on her own. She appreciated how he treated her. She found his way much less stressful than Reuben's hovering, take-charge methods.

She felt a moment's unease over Reuben. She shouldn't think poorly of him for it. Reuben, no doubt, felt responsible for her injuries, since the accident had happened while he was taking her home.

Meg paused to watch as her mother put the cake into the back of the buggy. Then she started carefully down the porch steps, with Peter close behind her. She wavered and nearly lost her footing, but his quick grip on her arm steadied her. *"Danki,"* she murmured, overly aware of his strength.

"You want me to carry you like Reuben does?" he teased.

She felt her face heat. *"Nay!"*

He was silent a long moment. "I didn't think so." His tone was dry.

Feeling foolish, Meg negotiated the rest of the way to his buggy. Without asking, Peter grabbed her crutches and set them in the vehicle. He then caught her about the waist and lifted her easily onto the front seat, before going around to slide in next to her. They waved to her mother as they left.

Bishop John Fisher's house wasn't far, less than ten minutes at a canter. Peter kept his gaze fixed on the road as he steered the vehicle. His continued silence after several minutes made Meg antsy. They'd gotten along so well during their last meeting. Had something changed? Was it because of Wednesday's outing?

She heard him sigh. "I hope John agrees to the party. If not, I don't know what we'll do."

"We'll have to find a way to convince him," Meg said.

He flashed her a smile. "You're determined. I like that. Will you do the talking, or should I?"

She responded to his good humor with a smile. "We both will."

"Who should go first?" he teased.

Her lips twitched. "You can." Meg relaxed as the tension between them dissipated.

Peter flipped on the battery-operated blinker and made a right turn. "When do you go get your cast off?" His tone was conversational.

"After four weeks. The doctor said it normally takes six weeks for a broken leg to heal. I don't think mine will take longer."

"Four weeks… That would be the week of the party."

"Ja." She sighed, annoyed by the weight of her cast.

"Do you know what the doctor will do?" Peter steered the horse onto the bishop's road.

"He'll want to do X-rays to see how my leg is healing."

Peter was quiet as he parked near Bishop John's barn. "I can take you to the doctor's if you want." He hesitated. "And to physical therapy when you need it."

She got a funny feeling in her stomach. *"Danki,* Peter. That's kind of you. If I need you to take me, I'll let you know." She felt her cheeks warm.

Peter jumped out of the buggy and came around to help her.

"I wonder who's here," Meg murmured as she spied two other vehicles in the barnyard. "I hope we don't have to postpone our conversation with him."

"We'll stop in to visit, and if we can't talk, we'll give him the baked goods, then come back another time."

Peter assisted her from the buggy, then waited for her to precede him around the vehicle toward the house. Meg exchanged glances with him as he joined her. He rapped on the wooden door. When no one answered, he tried again. This time the door opened, revealing a familiar young woman with Bishop John's baby son, Nicholas, on her hip.

"Peter!" she cried.

"Sally," he answered warmly. "I'm surprised to see you here."

His cousin shrugged. "It was my turn to come." She pushed the door open and stepped back to allow them to enter. "*Hallo*, Meg." She eyed her and Peter carefully.

"*Hallo*, Sally." Meg shot Peter a look. Sally Hershberger was not only Peter's cousin; she was the daughter of Alta Hershberger, the busybody of their church community. Could they trust Sally with their party plans? His aunt Alta had never been able to keep a secret.

"I'm surprised to see the two of you."

"We're not together," Meg said quickly. Too quickly, she realized, when she felt Peter stiffen beside her.

"Nay," he agreed. "We've got something we'd like to discuss with John."

At his tight tone, Meg shot him a glance, but his expression was unreadable as he explained the reason for their visit. She tensed as she stood with him in the hallway. She felt as if she'd offended him, and that hadn't been her intention.

"John's in the back room," Sally told them as she moved down the hall. "I'll tell him you're here."

Meg felt the air between her and Peter turn chilly as they waited. "I'm sorry. Peter, I didn't mean—"

"It was nothing, Meg. You told the truth. We're not together." His words shocked her and made her feel awful. She could only hope they could get back to their friendly working relationship.

"Sally's not like her *mam*, is she? She won't tell anyone why we've come?"

She heard him sigh. "*Nay*, she's not like Alta. She's suffered because of her mother's tendency to natter. She'll not say a word."

After a long moment of silence, Meg said, *"Gut."* She felt awkward. She was pretty sure their easy working relationship had been tested by her earlier comment. And she should have kept her mouth shut about his cousin, she realized with regret.

Sally returned within moments. "Come on back." Her voice grew soft, but her eyes held sadness. "I think he's searching for a reason to be thankful." She bit her lip. "He spent Thanksgiving alone—him and Nicholas." She opened her mouth. "I wanted to come and cook for him, but he didn't want to keep me from my family. I would have invited him to the *haus*, but *Mam*…"

Meg felt a rush of sympathy. "How was your Thanksgiving?"

"It was fine." Sally smiled shyly, and Meg stared, stunned by the beauty in her expression. Meg thought that the young woman looked like a natural mother, with the bishop's baby son clearly happy in her arms. But she knew that Sally had never married, and as far as she knew, there wasn't any sweetheart in the picture.

They followed Sally to a small room off the main living area. John sat at a table, his attention on the piece of paper before him as he scribbled on it with a pencil.

"John," Sally said softly.

The bishop looked up. "Peter. Meg." He rose from his chair and moved into the larger room. Meg and Peter joined him, each taking a seat across from him.

Meg wondered if he felt more encumbered by his position in the church now that his wife was dead. Catherine Fisher had been ill and frail since the birth of their son. On the day his wife had collapsed and died, John had learned that she'd developed a serious heart problem. He'd been chosen by the church elders. He would be the bishop in charge of their church district until the day he died. It was both a blessing and a curse to be selected as bishop. Most community men didn't want the position. But John had taken it and done a good job. Still, Meg could see the tired lines around his soft brown eyes and the deep sadness there. She could only imagine what it felt like to lose someone you loved, someone who meant the world to you.

"Sally said you wanted to talk with me."

Meg hesitated and flashed Peter a glance.

"We have a favor to ask of you, John," Peter began. He explained that his father and her mother wanted to give their spouses a special surprise birthday celebration, and that Arlin and Miriam both had Christmas birthdays.

"And you need me for?"

Meg bit her lip. "We were hoping you'd allow us to hold the party here."

John looked surprised—and understandably leery. "I don't know." He appeared lost, like a young boy unsure of facing the world after a terrible disappointment.

"I know it's a huge imposition, but we'd handle everything." She softened her expression as she took in his hesitation. John had grown thinner since Catherine had died, and she hated to see him that way. She wondered why the Lord provided someone to love and spend the rest of his life with, only to take her home, leaving a grief-stricken man to raise his child alone. As people of God, their Amish community took comfort in the fact that their deceased loved ones were at home with the Lord, but that didn't necessarily make it easier for those who still grieved.

The bishop rubbed a hand across his forehead. "I don't—"

"John," Peter said, his voice soft and filled with compassion, "wouldn't it be better to spend the holiday with us, surrounded by our church community, people who care about you, than to spend it alone in this house all by yourself with only Nicholas for company?"

"The decision is yours." Meg rose, warmed by the gentle way Peter spoke to him. Still, she knew the man needed time to mull over their request. "Will you please think about it? We'll come back another time. We don't want to pressure you."

Peter stood on cue. "If there is anything you need me to do, will you call on me?" He paused. "Are your horses ready for the winter? I heard there is a possibility of snow in the next few days."

John looked surprised, as if he hadn't considered that he might need to do anything for his horses before the worst of the winter weather rolled in. "I think they're *oll recht*."

"I can check them if you'd like, before we leave," Peter offered.

The bishop nodded. "I'd appreciate that. *Danki*."

Sally showed them out. "I think it's a wonderful idea—having your parents' party here," Peter's cousin said.

"He has the space, and we figured it would help him, too."

Sally nodded as she led the way through the kitchen. "He needs all the help he can get." Without conscious thought, it seemed, she ran her fingers lovingly through Nicholas's soft, baby-fine hair. "This poor boy needs his *dat*. John manages to take care of him at night, but during the day he seems too lost to pay much attention to him." She frowned. "I don't mean he's not a *gut vadder*, because he is. He's just grieving so."

"The churchwomen will be pushing for him to marry soon," Meg said.

"Ja," the other woman said. "Nicholas needs a *mudder."* She gazed at the baby with longing. Then she blushed, as if embarrassed. She quickly shuttered her expression and her lips curved. "So you will be back to get his answer?"

"Ja," Peter said. "You'll not tell your *mam*?"

"You have to ask?" Her laughter was harsh. "It wouldn't be a surprise party if I told her. You don't have to worry about me telling my *mudder* anything." She scowled. *"Mam* is pushing me to wed, and she's decided on John. It seems she thinks I'll make a *gut* second wife for him."

"I'm sorry," Peter said, eyeing his cousin with concern.

Studying her, Meg suspected that Sally would love to be John's wife and a mother to his son, but she was afraid that with her *mam's* interference, she'd lose her chance at happiness. Meg didn't doubt that Alta's methods would hurt rather than help Sally's future with the kind bishop.

"Ach, nay, I nearly forgot," Peter said, as his gaze settled on Nicholas's wooden high chair, which was pushed close to the kitchen table. "The food." He glanced at Meg. "Wait here," he said. "I'll be right back."

Meg nodded. Her gaze went to Sally. "That little boy thinks the world of you," she murmured.

Sally beamed. "He's a sweet baby. I just wish…"

"Ja?" Meg waited a heartbeat before finishing her sentence. "That he could be more to you?"

"I wish he could be, but the likelihood of that is close to zero chance."

"Why do you say that?" Meg readjusted the crutches under her arms.

"I'm sorry," the woman said. "Please sit down. Your leg must be bothering you."

"It's getting better." She stared down at her cast as she eased into a kitchen chair. "I can't wait to get it off, but it will be a while yet." She returned her gaze to Sally. "You like him. The bishop."

"And he still loves his wife."

"She's gone," Meg reminded her.

"But he can't get past her memory. And for me to have a chance? With my *mam*, there's not much of one." Sally sighed. "I love my *mudder*. I know how devastated she was after my *vadder* passed. She's been a *gut mam* despite her tendency to…"

"Talk?" Meg suggested.

Sally agreed, her lips turning up in a smile. "I'd love to be here for John and Nicholas. I'm trying to be here for them, but when there are many women who want to see their daughters wed to a man as kind and caring as John is, it's hard to have hope."

"How often do you come here to help out?"

"As often as I can." She shifted the little boy in her arms. "And we have a *gut* time together, don't we, Nicholas?" The baby patted her cheek as if he understood.

"Do the other daughters come?" Meg couldn't think of which women had the other daughters.

Sally shrugged. "Some, but not many and not often. 'Tis been the older women who have been taking a turn, but since I don't have a family of my own, they usually accept the fact that I can be here more often than they can." She was quiet a moment. "I guess they don't believe I have a chance with him."

Meg studied Sally, who was lovely, with soft brown hair and light blue eyes. "I hope you get it all, Sally. I'll pray for it."

Delight spread on the girl's face. "*Danki*, Meg. I heard that Reuben Miller wants to court you. I hope he makes you happy."

Her words made Meg feel awful for what she'd said earlier—jumping to deny the fact that she and Peter were a couple. Rejecting him. "About earlier. Peter and I are…"

"Working together as friends."

Meg nodded. "*Ja*, we've found a way to be friends."

Sally nodded. *"Gut."* She appeared to search for words. "He liked you for a long time."

"He did?" She didn't believe her. She'd cared for him once, too, until she'd overheard what he'd said, and she'd confronted him later that same day.

"*Ja*, but I understand that you want Reuben. And I'm glad you've found a way for you and Peter to get along."

Peter came into the house with the cake and two loaves of bread. He grinned as he set them on the kitchen table. "From my *mudder* and Meg's."

"Danki," Sally said. "That will save me from baking today and tomorrow."

Peter raised his eyebrows. Meg, hoping to spare Sally any discomfort, quickly suggested they leave. "You did say you had to work in the shop today," she reminded him.

Peter politely held the door open for her as Meg hobbled outside, down one step toward the carriage. She paused as something occurred to her, then halted and faced him. "Did your *mam* know why you were coming to see the bishop?"

"She baked for him. She's the one who wanted me to come." His grin was noticeably absent. "She knows nothing about our plans."

Meg felt something inside tighten and clench. She'd hurt him again, and she hadn't meant to.

He was courteous as he helped her into his buggy, but then was quiet on the ride back, until he pulled up close to the house. He got out and came around to the left side of the vehicle.

"I guess we'll give John a few days before we check back about the party."

She nodded, fighting tears.

He held out his hand and helped her down. "Take care, Meg," he said, his voice overly polite.

"Bye, Peter." And despite the fact that she knew she'd see him again regarding the party, Meg felt as if it was really a goodbye to the camaraderie bordering on friendship they'd discovered since their first planning meeting.

After Peter left, Meg moved through the house toward the kitchen.

"*Gut*, you're back!" *Mam* said as she turned from the stove. "I've got lunch almost ready." She looked behind her and frowned. "Where's Peter?"

"He had to get to the shop." Meg felt worse than ever. She and Peter had been getting along and now she'd offended him. Again. When the only thing she wanted was for him to like her. She should have kept her mouth closed after seeing Sally's surprise at seeing her and Peter together. Why hadn't she? Because she didn't want to be courted by Reuben Miller, she realized.

She wanted Peter Zook.

Chapter Nine

Peter decided to stop at Agnes's before he headed to his father's blacksmith shop. Meg's quick denial to Sally's comment about them being together bothered him. He felt raw, and he needed to see his friend, to be soothed by her friendship and kind humor. She and her sister were outside hanging clothes on the line when he pulled up to their house.

He parked, got out and approached without their knowledge. They were too far out in the yard to have heard his buggy. He felt his lips curve as he jogged across the grass. "Agnes!"

She turned. Her eyes widened as she grinned. "Peter!" She met him halfway. "What are you doing here?"

"Came to see you, since I didn't get to stop by on Thanksgiving."

Agnes didn't look the least bit upset. "It was a busy day, what with my cousins' arrival late the night before." She waved to the other young woman who watched them from near the clothesline. "Lydia!" she called. "Come meet Peter."

The girl who Peter had thought was Alice advanced.

As she drew near, he saw that she was much younger than Alice. While she was blonde like Agnes and her twin sister, she had dark brown eyes instead of light blue ones.

Agnes grabbed his hand as she made introductions. Lydia smiled shyly as she regarded him curiously. She wore a lavender dress with a black coat. She was pretty, but Peter thought Agnes and Meg were prettier. He frowned. The last person he should be thinking about was Meg Stoltzfus.

"Will you eat with us?" Agnes asked a few moments later.

"Sorry, but I can't. I have to work in the shop today." He couldn't keep from smiling at both girls. Agnes's good mood was a soothing balm to his battered defenses. It had been easy to become fast friends with her when she'd come with her sister and brother to the youth singing in his church community, where they'd met. Now he was determined that they become more.

"Are you coming to our church service on Sunday?" he asked.

Agnes shook her head. "Not this Sunday. *Mam* wants us to attend church service in our own community, with our family in from out of town."

Peter nodded. "Lydia, how many siblings do you have?"

"Five older brothers and a younger sister."

When his eyes widened, the girl laughed. "*Ja*, five older brothers. You would be kind to a *schweschter, ja*?"

"*Ja.* I've got two sisters and I'm kind to them. Annie is married. Barbara isn't." He frowned as he thought of Barbara. She'd been staying with relatives in New Wilmington for over a year. At one time, he'd thought that Barbara and Preacher Levi would marry, but something had happened between them. And then Barbara had left. It had been too long since his family had seen her.

"Do you want to come to our Sunday services?" Agnes asked, drawing his attention.

Peter thought about it, then quickly rejected the idea. It would be nice to spend time with Agnes without tension or concerns, but he still had a party to plan with Meg. And he had to find a way to work with her again. "I can't this week." He smiled to show that he would have liked to go.

"Are you going to the singing?"

Peter nodded. "You want me to come get you?" he offered. He couldn't take all of Agnes's cousins, but he could take Agnes, Alice and Lydia.

Agnes beamed at him. "That would be *wunderbor*."

"I need to get to the shop." He made arrangements to pick up the twins and Lydia Sunday evening before the youth singing. Agnes seemed fine with attending the one in his community despite the fact that there would be one in hers, as well.

"We'll see you on Sunday, Peter," Lydia said quietly.

He nodded, then left, hurrying as he realized the time—he should have been hard at work in his father's blacksmith shop by now.

Reuben surprised Meg with a visit later that afternoon, after Peter had dropped her off and she'd eaten lunch with her family.

"Reuben!" she exclaimed, when Ellie ushered him into the room. "I didn't expect to see you today."

"I hope it's *oll recht* that I've come. 'Tis been a while since I've seen you."

"I'm glad you came," Meg said sincerely. After the way Peter had left her abruptly, it felt good to have someone genuinely happy to see her. *Peter*, she thought. *Why is it always so difficult to deal with Peter?*

"Sit down, Reuben," her mother said warmly. "Would you like a piece of apple pie?"

He smiled. "*Ja*, that would be nice, Missy." He chose the seat across from Meg, who regarded him with affection. "'Tis *gut* to see you, Meg."

"You've been working hard, I hear," she said. The crew he worked with was apparently trying to get a commercial building done before winter rolled in full force.

The good humor left his face as he regarded her with concern. "Meg, I won't be able to make Sunday's youth singing. My *eldre* wants us to visit my *grossmudder* in Millersburg."

Meg knew of the Amish community. "I didn't know your *grossmammi* lived in Ohio."

"*Ja.*" He seemed to relax. "I have an aunt, an uncle and lots of cousins there."

"That will be nice for you to see them." She was pleased for him. Family was important. Her father had taught her that.

"*Ja.*" He seemed to study her, as if trying to gauge her reaction about his absence.

"Reuben, you're not worried I'm upset that you're leaving?"

He waited a heartbeat. "I am. I care about you, Meg. I don't want you to think differently."

"I know, Reuben. And I believe you." She wished she could feel more excited about his serious interest in her. Her lips curved. "When do you go?"

"In two hours."

"It was nice of you to stop by and let me know."

He reached for her hand across the table. Fortunately, there was no one in the room besides them. She should have withdrawn her fingers, but Reuben was clearly upset to be leaving her.

Yet, she wasn't. And why was that? She didn't want to think about it too closely.

"Meg, I'll come see you when I get back." His touch was warm, but it didn't make her tingle like…Peter's.

"Will you be gone a week?"

"Three days," he told her. "*Dat* has hired a driver to take us."

She understood why. The distance was too far to travel by buggy.

"Will you miss me?"

"Of course." *As a friend and nothing more*, she thought. Reuben was a kind, thoughtful man, but she'd been unsure about her feelings for him since they'd started to see each other. Since he'd saved her from drowning the night of the accident, she'd made a silent promise to give their relationship a chance.

She had a mental vision of Peter and quickly fought to banish it.

Reuben grinned, then stood. Her mother entered the room. "Don't you want your pie?" she asked him.

"May I take it with me? We're leaving for Ohio in a couple hours."

Mam wrapped up Reuben's pie, and the man left shortly afterward. "That was nice of him to stop by before he left."

"*Ja*, it was." Meg knew Reuben was a kind and thoughtful man. She just had to decide whether or not he was the right man for her.

Sunday arrived quickly, and the family left for church services at the William Mast farm. As they neared the property, Meg saw several buggies ahead of theirs and knew them to belong to other church community members.

As she climbed the steps to the door leading to Josie Mast's kitchen, Meg saw Josie's daughter Ellen talking with Annie Lapp, Peter's sister. On the other side of the room, her aunt Katie stood with Meg's friend Martha, who was her cousin Eli's wife. Meg carefully negotiated the three steps onto the porch. Catching sight of her, Ellen rushed forward to open the door.

"Meg!" she said in greeting. "You're looking so much better."

Meg smiled. "I feel better." She glanced around the room, noting other familiar female faces within her community. "*Mam's* outside. We've brought cheesecake and German potato salad."

The other woman's eyes gleamed. "I love German potato salad."

"Where's my cousin?" Meg teased.

"Which one?" But Ellen blushed, so Meg knew she understood that she meant Isaac, Ellen's sweetheart. "He's outside in the barn."

"I like him for you," Meg said, and the young woman beamed at her. "Can I do anything?"

Have you seen Peter? she wanted to ask, but didn't. She couldn't allow others to know they were working together, but since Peter had left without their making any plans to meet again, she'd have to find a way to talk with him without anyone guessing.

"There you are, Meg," Annie said as she approached. She held her daughter, Susanna, on her hip. Her four-year-old son was absent, no doubt with his father, Meg thought. "Did you happen to see Peter outside?"

Meg shook her head. "*Nay.* I didn't see anyone out in the yard except those of us who just arrived." Which included Alta and Sally Hershberger and the Abram Peachys. *Peter is here*, she thought. Suddenly, she felt nervous. Could she find some way to smooth things over between them so they could continue to work together? She hoped so.

She wondered if he'd be going to the singing tonight. If he did, he would go with Agnes. Reuben wasn't here, so she should probably stay home. But did she want to?

She didn't see Peter until church service began. Furniture had been removed from the Masts' great room. Since it was November, the service would be inside the house rather than the barn, where there was more space. She spied him seated next to her cousin Jacob. Peter held EJ in the men's section. The smaller children often sat with their mother, but EJ had become a well-behaved little boy who clearly enjoyed his uncle's attention.

Meg was unable to look away from them. She had arrived before the men and was seated between Martha and Leah. As if sensing her regard, Peter met her gaze. She tried to smile, but found she couldn't. He didn't look happy with her, and could she blame him? *Nay, I can't.*

The service proceeded as usual—with over two hours of singing, preaching and more hymns. Soon, Preacher Levi Stoltzfus—who was no relation to Meg—finished speaking, and everyone started to leave the room. The men headed outside, while the women started to get the midday meal ready to be served indoors.

Meg rose on her crutches and headed toward the kitchen. Then she stopped and sighed. There wasn't anything she could do to help. She couldn't carry food and walk with crutches at the same time.

The kitchen was filled with happy chatter and women pulling covers off cold food items. Meg sat down in a chair, leaned the crutches against the wall, then reached across the table to uncover her sister's German potato salad.

"I'll take that," Annie said, as she pulled the uncovered bowl toward the edge of the table. She handed Meg her two-year-old daughter. "Will you hold her?"

Meg smiled. "I'll be happy to." She settled Susanna on her lap across her uninjured leg. "*Hallo*, little one. Are you hungry?"

The child nodded vigorously.

"Anything special you hope to eat?"

"Pie."

She arched her eyebrow. "Pie? No cake or cookies? Just pie?"

"Cho-co-lit," Susanna said, nodding. "And appa-sauce."

"That's a fine idea. I like applesauce and chocolate."

The toddler grinned, and Meg felt her heart melt. There was something so sweet about a child's smile. When Susanna looked at her with approval, she felt as if her whole world brightened with the sun. Holding the little girl in her arms, smelling her clean baby scent made Meg long to have a baby of her own. She tried to envision her child. She was unable to picture one with blond hair and blue eyes. Meg drew a sharp breath. She could see her daughter with dark hair and gray eyes...

Nay! She wouldn't allow herself to fall for him again. She'd done it once, and it hadn't worked out well. Thankfully, Peter hadn't had a clue that she'd had a crush on him.

Peter. She had to finish planning this party with him. In order to do so, they would have to meet again—and soon. Christmas was only four weeks away, and they had yet to get Bishop John's answer on whether or not they could use his house for the celebration.

Meg sat, enjoying the little girl as the other women of the community unwrapped and set out all the food in the other room. The men would eat first, so she stayed where she was while Josie Mast went to let the men know that their meal was ready.

She heard them come in through the main door. The sound of deep young male tones, intermingled with older, more mature and masculine voices, filtered into the kitchen from the main room.

"Would you like me to take her?" Annie asked, stepping back to see how Meg was faring with her daughter.

"We're fine, aren't we, Susanna?"

The child nodded. "*Gut, Mam.* Meg's going to have cho-co-lit pie, too. And appa-sauce."

Annie laughed as she and Meg exchanged amused glances. "She is, is she?"

"Ja." Susanna frowned. "Where's EJ?"

"He's with *Dat*," her mother said.

The child's lip quivered. "I want to be with *Dat*."

"'Tis the men's turn to eat, *dochter*. You'll have to eat with me." She paused. "And Meg."

Meg nodded. "*Ja*, we'll get to eat applesauce and pie together. And other things, as well."

"Lots of pie?" Susanna asked.

"Plenty for a little girl just your size," Meg assured her, and was pleased when Annie shot her a grateful look.

The men finished their meal and, despite the cold, moved outside to the barn, where they often had discussions about their farms, the weather and other topics that interested them. Annie came for her daughter and Meg rose, grabbed her crutches and followed the two into the next room more slowly. There was plenty of food left on tables against the two walls. Meg saw

Annie get Susanna situated before fixing her a plate of food. Smiling, Meg hobbled toward the seat next to the child, until she saw Peter crouched down beside his niece. His expression was warm and loving as he spoke with her. Susanna clearly loved her uncle, if her beaming expression was any indication.

Her heart beating wildly, Meg froze. Peter looked up, saw her and abruptly stood. He bent to say something to Susanna that made her laugh. Suddenly anxious, Meg felt her face heat. *Did he say something about me?* She swallowed hard and continued her awkward approach.

"Mee!" Susanna cried, warming her heart. "Seat!"

Continuing forward, praying she didn't trip and fall, Meg moved toward the little girl and her now-silent uncle.

"*Hallo*, Peter," she said, as she tried to maneuver into the chair that Annie and her daughter had saved for her.

"Meg." He pulled it out and helped her to sit.

She blushed, wondering why she was embarrassed by his thoughtfulness now, when he'd helped her before without her feeling awkward. She thanked him quietly and he started to move away. "Peter," she called softly. He halted and glanced back. "Will we…" she began.

He nodded.

"Monday?" she suggested.

He remained silent too long.

"Monday what?" Annie asked, as she walked up.

"Tomorrow is Monday," Peter said. "And it may snow."

Annie frowned.

Meg thought quickly. "I was hoping that Peter would come early to check on our horses. You know, with winter coming…"

His sister's brow cleared. "*Ja*, you and Jacob have been busy," she said.

"If you're too busy…" Meg said.

"'Tis no problem. We're nearly caught up."

"*Ja*, Meg, he'll be happy to come." Annie turned her daughter's plate so that the applesauce was directly in front of her. "Better than waiting until after the first snowfall."

"I heard it will snow this week." Meg avoided Peter's gaze.

"I'll be over tomorrow," he promised.

She looked at him then, saw nothing in his expression that suggested he was still angry with her.

"I'll let you eat your meal," he said, then left.

"Look!" Susanna said. "I've eaten all my appa-sauce." She pouted. "You don't have any food yet."

Leah came up to the table and set a plate before Meg. "Let me know if there's anything else you'd like," she said.

"Appa-sauce," Susanna exclaimed. "And cho-co-lit pie." She grinned up at Meg's sister. "We're supposed to eat it together."

Amusement entered Leah's expression. "I'd better get her some of both then," she declared.

As she regarded Susanna, smiling in turn, Meg suddenly felt as if she was being watched. She glanced up and saw Peter in the doorway, staring at her. She blinked and wondered what he was thinking. Tomorrow they'd talk, and she would apologize. Except, did she have anything to apologize for? As he'd said, she and Peter weren't together—not as a couple, but they were as a party-planning team.

She gave him a smile, and something shifted in his expression before he turned abruptly and left the house.

"Here you go," Leah said, putting another smaller plate before her.

"Danki," she murmured. But as she picked up her spoon to try her applesauce, she found that she was too tense to eat—until Susanna started to chat nonstop. Then Meg found herself relaxing and purposely put the child's uncle from her thoughts.

Tomorrow would be soon enough to deal with Peter Zook.

Chapter Ten

The next day Peter was on his way to see Meg when he spied a puppy on the side of the road. The little dog was injured, and while he knew he had to get to Meg's, he pulled his buggy over and parked. The animal was a tiny thing, with lots of fur. He approached carefully and it moved, lifting its little head to gaze up at him with sad eyes.

He felt something shift inside him. He couldn't leave the dog there. The animal needed medical care. He'd have to take it to James Pierce, Meg's brother-in-law and a veterinarian.

He removed the quilt his family kept under the front seat of the buggy, spread it on the ground close to the dog and carefully reached for the animal, silently praying it didn't bite or snap at him. He eased his hands closer, then slipped them under its body. The dog whimpered but didn't strike out. He picked it up and eased it gently onto the quilt. Then he wrapped up the dog loosely, like swaddling a baby, with only its head visible above the fabric. Peter placed the animal on the floor in front, then grabbed the leathers and began the journey to Meg's.

His first thought had been to take the dog directly to the veterinarian, then to send word to Meg why he didn't show. But that would only make things more difficult between them, so he drove on to her place so he could explain the situation and she could see the dog for herself.

It didn't take long to reach the Arlin Stoltzfus residence. Peter left the dog in the buggy while he hurried up the steps and knocked on the door. No one answered, so he tried again. After what seemed like a long time, the door opened, revealing Meg on her crutches.

"Peter, glad you could make it," she said hesitantly.

"I can't stay," he said. He saw her face fall. "Meg, I've got an injured dog in my buggy. I found him on the side of the road."

Her brow cleared. "May I see him?"

He held the door open for her as she came out onto the porch.

"What happened to him? Do you know?"

He stayed right behind Meg as she moved down the steps. She was using the crutches much better now, as if she'd become used to them as an extension of her.

"*Nay*, but I'd guess that he was hit by a car." The dog wasn't bloody, but Peter wondered if that was a good or bad thing. If it had been hit by a car, the little dog could be suffering internal injuries. The only thing that gave him hope was that the animal had opened its eyes once and looked at him.

They reached the buggy at the same time. Peter opened the door.

"Aww," Meg breathed. "Poor thing."

He was stunned by the softness in her expression. This was a totally different side of Meg. Not that he hadn't seen her smile—with someone else—or heard her laugh. He recalled with startling clarity the day they'd each announced their choice of party location. The fact that they'd agreed had shocked them both. The feeling he'd experienced that day had buoyed his spirits and given him hope that he and Meg could work well together.

"I thought I'd take him to James."

Meg met his gaze, her blue eyes shining. "*Ja,* that is a *gut* plan." She bit her lip, as if she'd had an idea but was afraid to suggest it.

"But?" he asked gently, encouragingly.

"What if you put him in our barn? We can have James come here. Now that Nell is married, the stall where she kept Jonas and Naomi is empty. It's a nice space, and he'll be safe there."

Peter looked at the dog, then returned his attention to Meg. "That's a fine plan."

She seemed relieved. "I wish I could hold him."

He softened his expression as he eyed her thoughtfully. "He's a little thing. I'm sure I can manage to carry him on my own."

"Oh, I didn't mean—"

"Meg," he said quickly, "I'm teasing you."

She stared at him a moment, then he saw her relax. "I'm sorry, but I seem to be on tenterhooks here."

"Meg, 'tis *oll recht.*" He reached inside and picked up the quilt-wrapped dog. "He's so small. I hope there's nothing seriously wrong." He cradled the animal against his body.

"I hope so, too." Meg was eyeing the dog with obvious sorrow and longing. "Come, I'll show you where to put him."

She started toward the barn, then flashed him a smile

over her shoulder that made him inhale sharply. "It's a boy?"

His lips curved slightly. "Not sure. I didn't pay much attention to anything but that he's hurt and I want to help."

She paused at the barn door. "You're a *gut* man, Peter Zook."

Her words stunned him into silence.

Despite her crutches, Meg managed to open the door and lead the way. She walked down the aisle to a stall, unlatched the door and gestured inside. "I know it might not seem like much." She bit her lip, and he found himself fascinated by the nervous gesture. "But Jonas and Naomi were happy here. I think this little one will be, too, once Nell and James are here to help him."

Peter entered the stall and hunkered down to set the dog on a bed of straw. "This is a *gut* space, Meg. Sheltered and with straw to keep him warm. He'll do well here. Now we just have to get Nell and James to come." He stroked the dog's back for a minute, then rose to his feet.

"Ellie is due home any minute. She has a cell phone. We can use it to call James." Meg looked as if she wanted to pet and hold the puppy. "We wouldn't have been able to stay here to make plans."

He arched his eyebrow. "I see."

She blushed. "*Nay*, Peter, you don't. I didn't know that she'd be back. I just found the note she left my *mudder. Mam's* not home, either. 'Tis just me today." Concern laced her voice. "I didn't have a way to let you know."

He softened his expression. "'Tis fine. Everything worked out for the best, *ja*?"

He heard her release a heavy sigh. "I suppose so."

She turned her attention back to the dog. "Should we give him water?"

"Sure. We don't know if he'll drink it, but he may be thirsty. I don't know how long he was lying there."

Meg smiled. "I'll get him some." She moved from the stall and hobbled down the length of the barn.

Peter hurried after her. "Meg, wait!"

She stopped and turned. *"Ja?"*

He was reluctant to continue. "May I carry it for you?" His gaze fell to her crutches.

Meg scowled. *"Ja,* that would be *gut.* Can't do much with these things." She was obviously frustrated.

He reached her side. "'Tis *oll recht,* Meg. You'll soon heal and be able to do all the things you did before." He fought the urge to caress her cheek.

She nodded, then pointed toward the bowls on a workbench against the wall directly in front of them. "The blue one is Jonas's bowl—we keep it here for when we watch Jonas and Naomi. The little one can use it."

Peter reached for the bowl and went outside to the pump to fill it. When he returned, he found Meg still standing there, staring into space. "What's wrong?" he asked.

She gasped. "I didn't see you come in." Her lips twisted. "I don't like being helpless."

"I'd hardly call you helpless, Meg. And we're planning a party together, which is work."

Her chuckle rang false. "Haven't gotten much done."

"We will," he assured her. "Today might have been a waste, but it will all come together."

Meg started back to the little dog's stall. "We need to check back with the bishop."

"Would you like me to do it on my way home?"

She was silent a long moment. *"Ja,* we have to know."

She hesitated before continuing. "When can we get together again?"

"When is a *gut* time for you?" He went inside the stall and set the water within the dog's easy reach. He gently unwrapped the quilt, giving the animal room to move. The dog opened its eyes and stretched its head toward the water bowl. Peter carefully picked him up so he could drink.

"Wednesday?"

He nodded as he gently lowered the animal to the quilt. He had things to do tomorrow. Wednesday would be a better day.

"What if my sisters are home?" Meg asked.

Satisfied that the dog was set for now, Peter stood and joined her outside the stall, making sure to close the door after him. "Then we'll find someplace else to work."

Meg appeared satisfied. "Wednesday then."

They made their way out of the barn. A buggy pulled into the barnyard and stopped as they exited the building. Ellie stepped out.

"Ellie!" Meg called.

Her sister turned to her. "*Hallo*, Meg." Her gaze widened as it settled on Peter as she approached. "*Hallo*, Peter."

"Ellie, do you have your cell phone with you?" Meg asked.

Her sister frowned. "*Ja*, why?"

"Would you please call James? Peter found an injured dog. He's in our barn."

"*Ja*, I'll call him." Ellie walked away from them to place the call. She talked animatedly as she spoke with either Nell or James, then returned a few minutes later. "They are on their way."

"*Danki*, Ellie," Peter said.

"May I see him?"

"*Ja*, I've put him in Jonas and Naomi's old space."

Ellie accompanied them to the barn. Peter watched Meg's sister as she entered the confined area and crouched beside the dog. "Did you say it was a he?" She regarded them with twinkling eyes. "Looks more like a she."

Peter laughed. "She it is. I didn't look too closely." He and Meg locked gazes. He regarded her with amusement, and to his surprise, she flashed him a grin. Her good humor made his stomach flutter.

Nell and James arrived minutes later. "We were in the area," Nell explained, as she and her husband stepped into the barn.

"He's in Jonas's old stall."

Nell smiled. "*Gut* place to put him." She spied the little dog on the quilt and her expression went soft. "Oh, look at him, James!"

James gazed at his wife with affection. "*Ja*, she's a pretty girl."

"Peter thought it was a he," Ellie teased.

Peter snorted. "I didn't care to look too closely."

James went into the stall and hunkered down beside his wife, who was stroking the little dog's head. "Shih Tzu," he said. When Nell met his gaze, he explained, "Her breed. Full grown." As he spoke, he tenderly maneuvered the little dog to examine her. "I don't see any external injuries."

"Could she have been hit by a car?" Peter asked.

"You say you found her by the side of the road?"

"*Ja*," he said. "When I went to get her, she looked up at me with big sad eyes. I had to help her."

Nell regarded Peter with approval. "You did the right

thing." She rubbed the animal's neck as her husband listened to the dog's belly with a stethoscope. "'Tis a good thing we were close by. If you'd brought her to the clinic, we would have missed you."

Peter gazed at Meg. "I'm glad I brought her here, too," he said quietly. Something flickered in Meg's expression before she averted her gaze. He felt a rush of warmth.

"I'm going to have to bring her home with us," James said. "I'll stop by the clinic first and ask Drew to x-ray her for me. We need to know if she has internal injuries."

Standing beside Meg and Ellie, Peter watched as Nell and James carefully picked up the little dog and carried her to their buggy. "You can come and see her later today if you'd like," Nell said. "I'll call Ellie and let her know how the little one's doing."

"She has no collar. Do you think we can come up with a name for her?" Meg eyed the dog longingly.

"What do you suggest?" Peter asked.

Meg was silent for a long moment. "How about Honey?" She blushed. "She looks like she's been sprinkled with wild honey."

"Honey," Nell murmured. "I like it."

"Me, too," James said, as he turned to study each of them. "We'll take *gut* care of Honey." Then he and Nell climbed into the buggy and left.

Ellie headed for the house. "I appreciate you calling them," Peter said to her.

"I'm glad I have a phone and could do it. Glad, too, that the church elders have given Nell and James permission to have one, too."

The elders of their church community allowed mobile phones under certain circumstances, such as for those who were in business. Ellie cleaned houses for the English, so she was granted one. James, the resident Amish veterinarian who treated farm animals and pets, was given another.

Ellie disappeared inside the farmhouse, leaving Peter and Meg alone.

They were quiet for several seconds. "I'll see you on Wednesday?" she asked tentatively.

Peter caught and held her gaze. "*Ja*. Will ten thirty be too late?"

"*Nay*, that will be fine." She teetered a bit on her crutches.

"You must be tired," he said with compassion. "'Tis a long time to stand on crutches, I imagine."

Meg sighed. "*Ja*, I am. I'll go in and lie down for a while after lunch." She studied the ground at her feet, and Peter had the impression that she was nervous for some reason. "Would you like to stay for lunch?"

"*Danki*, Meg, but I should get home." He smiled as she looked at him. "Remember, I want to stop at Bishop John's on the way. If he agrees, then we can continue with our plans. If not, I guess we'll be searching for another place to hold the party."

He headed toward his buggy, with Meg following. "I'll see you in the morning, Peter," she said.

He nodded, climbed into his buggy and steered the vehicle toward the road. She hadn't moved, but stood watching him, giving Peter a funny feeling inside his chest. He raised his hand to wave. She shifted her arm from her crutch and managed to wave back.

Tomorrow, they would sit down together like they had before. But for now Peter's head was filled with images of today: Meg's smile, her look of compassion for Honey, her nervous shifting.

He inhaled sharply and released the breath. *"Nay*, I must be imagining things. There is no reason for Meg to be nervous with me." She was seeing Reuben, and he was spending time with Agnes.

He readjusted his straw hat. "Meg Stoltzfus, we'll get the job done. Only four weeks to go. Surely, I can manage to spend a few hours in your company planning this party for your *vadder* and my *mudder*."

It shouldn't be too difficult. He hoped.

Meg watched Peter's departure before she returned to the house. Her heart fluttered as she recalled the way he'd been with Honey. He didn't seem to mind her name for the little dog. He no longer seemed upset with her, either, and she was glad. It meant they could work together again.

Would Bishop John agree to let them use his house? She didn't have a chance to ask on Sunday. John hadn't stayed after the service—which likely meant he was still unhappy and grieving.

Could Peter change his mind if John initially refused? She hoped so. She should try to think of another place just in case. But where? Where could they take their parents without them becoming suspicious?

She hobbled into the kitchen, where Ellie was pulling plates and glasses out for their midday meal. "May I help?"

Ellie turned. *"Ja*, if you'd like."

Meg grinned. "You're not going to insist I sit and rest?"

Her sister chuckled. "Would it make a difference if I did?"

"Nay." She set one crutch against the wall, then hob-

bled with the other toward the counter, where she picked up the plates. "*Gut* thing 'tis only you and me."

She set the table while Ellie took the fixings for sandwiches out of the refrigerator and pantry. They made their lunch, and Ellie poured them each a glass of milk.

"So," Ellie began, "Peter brought the dog to you."

Meg felt her face heat. "*Ja*. He found her just up the road, so he brought her here. He wanted to make sure it'd be *oll recht* to bring her to James."

"Hmm."

Meg narrowed her eyes. "What's that supposed to mean?"

"Only that he didn't continue on to Nell and James's *haus*."

"Because I knew you'd be home soon, and I thought it would be better for Honey if she stayed in the barn until Nell and James got here." She gazed at her sister, daring her to argue with her logic. "As it turns out, it's a *gut* thing you called them, since Peter would have wasted a trip with Honey to their place."

"True," Ellie agreed. She took a bite of her sandwich and swallowed. "Have you seen Reuben?"

"He's away. I expect him back in a day or two. Then he'll have to work, so I may not see him until the end of the week."

"Are you sure you like Reuben better than Peter?"

"Ellie!"

"'Tis a *gut* question, *ja*?" She took a sip of milk. "You can tell me. I won't tell a soul."

"Ellie…Peter is with Agnes now."

Ellie arched an eyebrow. "That's not what I asked."

"Reuben is a thoughtful, kind man. He'll make a *gut* husband."

"But is he the one you want?" her sister pressed.

Now that she was working with Peter, spending extra time with him, Meg felt pulled in two directions. She sighed, then said in a little voice, "I don't know."

Chapter Eleven

Meg sat on the exam table with her legs extended before her. Her mother waited in a chair. The doctor would be in soon with the results of her X-rays.

"I hope it's healing well," Meg murmured. "I can't wait to get this cast off. I want to be able to sleep upstairs again."

"You can sleep upstairs if you want. You've learned to use the crutches. It may be slow going up the steps, but I'm sure you'll manage."

"*Ja*, I suppose I could." But the thought of trying to maneuver up the stairs on crutches didn't sit well with her. She could hop on one foot all the way to the top landing, but what if she fell? Then she would be in worse shape than she was now.

The doorknob rattled, and the orthopedist the hospital had recommended entered the room. He was nice enough, but Meg didn't want to see him. She wanted to get over her leg injury and get back to her chores and her life.

"Well, Meg, I have your films," Dr. Reckling said. The man was middle-aged and wore a white lab coat over a white shirt and dark slacks. He slipped the X-ray films into the clip on the light. He flipped a switch, then gestured toward an area on her X-ray. "This is where you fractured the bone. It was a simple stress fracture, which is good. Do you see this?" He used his finger to outline a certain section. "It looks good. You're healing well, and because of this, I'm going to take off the cast and give you a brace instead." He turned to regard her with serious brown eyes. "You'll be able to take off the brace to shower, or to put up your leg for a short time, but, Meg, it's important that you wear it as much as possible. Do you understand?"

Meg was elated. She was getting the cast off! The fact that she'd have to wear a brace didn't bother her in the least. If she could shower without it, she was happy. "I understand," she said. "Will I be able to climb stairs in it?"

"You can if you're careful. You'll find the brace easier to get around on than this cast with crutches." His smile reached his eyes. "I'm sure you're sick and tired of those, aren't you?"

Meg nodded. "I'm eager to get rid of them."

"Let's do it now then." He reached into a cabinet and withdrew a small circular saw. Meg's eyes widened, and he laughed. "It won't hurt you. See?" He turned on the saw, then held it to his hand. "It vibrates and will cut the blue cast, but not the gauze underneath or your skin." He switched off the blade. "Are you ready?"

"I'm ready."

Less than half an hour later Meg and her mother were heading home. "How does it feel?" *Mam* asked.

"Different." In a way the boot seemed more cumbersome than the cast, but Meg figured it was just because she had to get used to it.

"Your *vadder* will be anxious to see you. He wanted to be the one to bring you, but he couldn't come. He'd promised to go with your *onkel* Samuel to see the bishop."

Meg blinked. Her father had gone to see the bishop? "Why?" She hoped John didn't say anything about their visit the other day. In the man's constant state of grief, what if he let it slip that she and Peter had stopped by?

"A repair to his house. Apparently, the glass is cracked in a back window, and with the colder weather here, it's been difficult to keep the house warm."

Forcing herself to relax, Meg asked, "Can they fix it in one day?"

"Ja," Mam said. "Samuel ordered a new piece of glass. They're going to replace the pane, not the window."

Praise be to God, Meg thought. It could be awkward if the bishop agreed to the party and she and Peter stopped over for planning purposes, and her father and her uncle were working on the premises.

"I'm glad *Dat* could help. I know *Onkel* Samuel's been busy lately. I heard Daniel has been working for the construction company that frequently employs Jed whenever he wants extra work."

"Ja, Isaac helps out there, too."

Meg liked living close to her father's family. But what of her mother? Did she regret moving so far from her parents and siblings? *"Mam?"*

Her mother put on the blinker and steered the buggy onto the road on the right. "Do you miss seeing your parents?" Meg asked.

"Sometimes, but not too often, because I have your *vadder*, you girls and Katie and her family." She was silent for a moment. "My *eldre* never approved of my choice to become Amish."

"Why?" Meg suspected she knew, but she wanted to hear her mother's side of things.

"They thought I should have the material things they enjoyed. I am happy with the life I've chosen, but I couldn't make them understand that."

"I'm sorry."

Mam smiled. "I'm not. There is nothing to be sorry for. I love you and your sisters. And if I had to relive my life, I'd marry your father again in an instant."

"I love you, *Mam*."

Her mother flashed a warm smile. "Love you, too, *dochter*. We're home!" She turned onto their dirt drive to park near the house, then ran around to help Meg.

"I can manage, *Mam. Danki.*" And she realized she could. Her foot and leg felt strange inside the boot rather than a cast, but she was able to get out of the buggy unaided. She grinned at her mother. "Looks like I'll be able to sleep upstairs in my own room tonight."

"I'll move my sewing things back downstairs."

As she started up the porch steps, the front door opened. To her surprise, in addition to her father stepping outside to greet her, Reuben was there as well, watching her with a bright light in his pale blue eyes.

"Why, *hallo*!" Meg greeted them. She raised her hand to halt Reuben after he started toward her. "I can manage." She saw his crestfallen look, and smiled to take the sting from her rejection.

Her father watched with approval as he waited for her to precede them indoors. "You're doing well, *dochter*," he murmured and she rewarded him with a grin.

"Let's eat. I don't know about you, but I'm hungry." Meg glanced back at Reuben. "You staying for lunch?"

It was kind of him to visit, and she was happy to spend time with him.

"*Ja*, I'd like that." He looked pleased by her invitation.

"*Gut*," her mother said. "It won't take me long to put food on the table."

"It won't take *us* long," Meg corrected as she headed toward the kitchen, where she planned to use her broader range of movement to help prepare lunch.

Peter parked near Meg's house and ran up the steps to the front door. There were no buggies in the yard, which meant there was a good chance she would be alone, except perhaps for her mother. He felt a flash of excitement as he knocked on the door.

"Come in!" someone called.

He opened the door, walked in and froze. Meg stood a few feet from him without crutches. He looked down, saw her medical boot and smiled. "You got your cast off."

She nodded but didn't return his smile.

"What's wrong?"

"Reuben is here."

Peter stiffened. "I didn't see his buggy."

She sent him an apologetic look. "His sister dropped him off. She'll be back for him soon, but..."

"I see." Peter felt his jaw tighten. "I'll go." He turned to leave.

"Peter," she said beseechingly, "you'll come back?"

He sighed and faced her. "In about an hour?"

She looked relieved. "*Ja*, that would be *gut*."

He nodded and hurried out the door before Reuben could see him and wonder why he was here. It bugged him that Reuben's visit took precedence over their planning meeting, but he couldn't find fault with Meg. Or could he? He told himself that he was over her and had moved on, but it still bothered him that she spent time with Reuben, the man she'd wanted for what seemed like forever, while he…

He ran around his buggy, climbed in and picked up the leathers. He had Agnes, he thought as he drove onto the road and made a right-hand turn. He might as well spend a little time with his nephew and niece, since he was over this way. He was sure Annie would be about ready for a break from her children right now.

Peter was able to push aside his bad humor as he thought about seeing EJ and Susanna, who meant a lot to him. The way they had taken to him from the first made him feel better. He pulled up alongside Annie and Jacob's house, got out, tied up his mare, then went to the back door.

"Honey, I'm home!" he called teasingly as he pushed the door slightly open.

Annie turned from the kitchen counter with Susanna perched on her hip. EJ was on the floor near her feet, playing with her pots and pans, making a racket as he beat on the bottom of a metal stockpot with a wooden spoon.

"Peter!"

He grinned. He was right. Annie was ready to be free of her beautiful children for just a few moments, until she could catch her breath. He rushed forward and took Susanna out of her arms. "Thought I'd stop over to spend time with my favorite *kinner*. *Hallo* there, Susie May."

"Pee-ter," she gushed, with an adorable baby-faced smile.

"*Onkel* Peter," her mother corrected.

"Her name is Susanna," EJ insisted. "Not Susie May."

"Her middle name is May," Peter pointed out.

"*Ja*, it is, EJ," Annie said. "Your *onkel* can call her anything he likes."

Peter gazed into the little girl's dark eyes, so like Jacob's. "Where is Jake? He's not at the shop, is he? I thought we got caught up yesterday."

"You did," Annie said, "until Aaron Troyer brought his four horses this morning. You know, the ones he uses for his buggy-ride business?"

"I didn't know." He frowned. How could he not know about the extra business? He'd talked with his father before heading over to Meg's. Then he realized that *Dat* must have thought it more important for him to meet with Meg than to work in the shop today. "I should go up to help."

"*Nay!* Please hang around until I get lunch prepared. It's been a bit of a difficult morning. Susanna is more clingy than usual, and EJ is feeling out of sorts. I'm afraid he's coming down with something."

Peter frowned. "EJ, come up here." He patted his right knee. Susanna was seated on his left one.

EJ didn't move. He pretended he hadn't heard his uncle, until Peter stared at him and said, "EJ, come sit on my lap." His second request was louder and more authoritative. Annie flashed him a look of approval. *"EJ."*

The little boy turned over the pot and dropped the wooden spoon inside with a clunk. He rose and approached Peter, who was instantly concerned when he saw his flushed cheeks. "Come up, buddy."

EJ climbed onto Peter's lap next to his sister. Peter reached around to feel the boy's forehead. "You're right, Annie. He feels feverish to me."

"I'm fine," the boy insisted.

"No, you're not. You have a fever." He rose with a child in each arm. "Do you have anything I can give him? Like aspirin? Maybe he should go to bed for a while."

"I don't need a nap," EJ complained.

"Not for a nap," Peter said. "For a story." He glanced at the kitchen wall clock and noted the time. He had forty-five minutes left before he had to return to Meg.

EJ perked up, clearly excited at the prospect of his uncle reading to him. "*Mam*, can I lie in bed for a story?"

Annie threw a casserole into the oven, then rose and faced her son. "You may."

Peter watched as his sister withdrew a small plastic bottle from a cabinet. Their grandmother's remedy for a fever had been to rub apple cider vinegar on the soles of their feet and on their palms. He hadn't known whether or not the vinegar helped. He only knew that he'd suffered through the awful smell because *Grossmammi* had insisted.

His other grandmother had used a different cure. She'd beaten the white of an egg with a spoon until it was foamy, then added a little sugar and some hot water, which she'd insisted he drink. He was glad that Annie used the more modern method for reducing a fever.

Annie gave her son two acetaminophen tablets, then Peter carried both children into the boy's bedroom. EJ stretched out on his quilt-covered bed, while his little sister cuddled against Peter's side.

"What story would you like to hear?" Peter hoped it was a quick one.

"*Dat* brought home a new book the other day," EJ announced as he adjusted the pillow under his head. "Will you read it? 'Tis called *May I Please Have a Cookie?*"

Peter found the book and began to read. He hid his delight in the way the children's author taught about using good manners through her story. When he finished reading, he saw that EJ had fallen asleep. Susanna, he realized, was also dozing in his arms. He stood with her and went into the living room, where he placed the sleeping child in a crib Annie kept there.

"They're both napping," he told his sister as he entered the kitchen.

She shot him a grateful smile. "Want some coffee?"

"*Nay*, I have errands to run. I just wanted to stop and visit."

Annie handed him a cookie. "You don't know how much it means to me that you love spending time with my children."

Peter shrugged. "They're my niece and nephew." He picked up his hat from where he'd set it on the table when he'd entered. "EJ is in his room, and Susie May is in her crib in the living room."

Annie's expression was soft as she watched him eat the cookie. "Again, *danki*."

He regarded her fondly. "My pleasure."

He left and headed back toward the Arlin Stoltzfus residence. What would he do if he got there and her father and sisters had returned?

He hesitated and considered going home, but he'd told Meg he'd be back in an hour, and he wouldn't break his word. The mental image of her floating in the water after the accident suddenly overwhelmed him. He felt his heart race and his stomach clench. Would he ever get that awful night out of his mind? He'd been able to control that memory for the most part, shoving it aside as if it hadn't made an impact on him. Had it returned when he'd learned that Reuben was in Meg's house? Reuben, who'd been driving, who had been injured along with Meg?

Agnes, he thought. He needed to see Agnes to remind himself that she was his future, and Meg was best left in his past. Which would be difficult, as long as he and Meg had to work together. But that was only for a few weeks more. The party date was fast approaching, which reminded Peter that they still had a lot to do. He shook away the horrible thoughts of the accident and used the rest of the drive to Meg's to focus on the party.

He smiled. As promised the day he'd found the dog, he'd stopped on his way home to check back with the bishop, and it looked as if John was going to allow them to use his house. Peter and Meg would visit him again to make sure. Sally hadn't been there when he had dropped by, but hopefully she'd be at John's today, and they could enlist her help if needed.

As he approached Meg's family's farmhouse, he saw a buggy parked next it. Reuben and his sister were outside, talking with Meg. The three were laughing, clearly enjoying themselves. Peter clenched his fingers around the reins and continued on. The sight of her looking so comfortable with Reuben and Rebekkah bothered him. It was as if she belonged in Reuben's world but not his. He and Meg were like oil and water at times. They didn't mix for long after being stirred.

He went to Whittier's Store and meandered about the aisles. He picked up a few things he knew his mother needed, and treats for EJ and Susanna. After paying for the items, he turned back toward Meg's. If Reuben was still there, he'd call it a day and go home.

It was half past twelve, and he was feeling hungry and out of sorts. He reached into his bag of purchases and withdrew a peanut butter candy bar. He quickly unwrapped it and took a bite, and the chocolate and peanut combination immediately made him feel better.

Until he thought of Reuben at Meg's house, and he scowled, the sweet treat now tasting bitter in his mouth.

Chapter Twelve

Meg looked pleased to see Peter as she opened the door and invited him in. "I wasn't sure you were coming back."

He tensed, then forced himself to relax. "I said I would." He paused. "Reuben get away *oll recht*?"

She appeared uncomfortable. "*Ja*, he left about fifteen minutes ago." She turned abruptly and walked into their living area, then gestured for him to sit. She sat some distance away, and it irritated him. "Did you see Bishop John?"

Peter nodded and forced himself to concentrate. "*Ja*, he's leaning toward allowing us to host the party there, but…"

"*Ja?* There's a but?"

"He didn't come right out and give his consent. I think we should visit him today and try again." He studied her concerned face and was drawn in by the deep blue of her eyes. His breath caught. "I think you can convince him. I'm willing to bet you can, in fact."

She seemed surprised by his comment. "You want to go now?"

"Is that a problem?"

"Nay," she assured him. "I'll let my mother know. She just stepped across the yard to see Mrs. Morgan, our neighbor."

Her *mam* had been home when Reuben was visiting. Something eased inside of Peter. He'd thought he'd heard her voice earlier, but he hadn't been sure.

"Would you like me to tell her for you?" he asked.

She beamed at him. "You don't mind?"

"Nay. I'll be happy to go. Just point me in the right direction."

After Meg explained that it was just next door, he hurried across the property to the house of the Englisher who lived there. He tapped on the door, and a woman immediately answered. "I'm sorry to bother you, but is—"

"Peter!" Missy was right behind her, as if she'd been preparing to leave.

"I came to let you know that Meg and I are heading over to Bishop John's."

Missy smiled. "I appreciate your telling me."

As Peter turned to run back, he heard Meg's mother say something to Mrs. Morgan, but he couldn't hear the words. He raced across the yard to Meg, who stood next to his buggy, waiting for him. Emotion rose up inside him at the sight of her. If only things were different between them…

He silently scolded himself as he slowed his approach, and calmed himself enough to smile at her as he reached the vehicle.

"Ready to go?" he asked.

She nodded. He stood close as she opened the door, grabbed hold of the side and placed her good foot inside the buggy. She attempted to heft herself up, but struggled and eventually stepped back.

"May I help?" He kept his voice soft. He knew she wanted to manage on her own.

She turned to give him a frustrated look.

"Wait! I have an idea." He ran to the barn and found a wooden crate he knew the Stoltzfus girls used for picking apples. When he returned, he saw Meg's eyes widen with delight. Peter placed it close to the carriage so that she had an extra step to make it easier for her to climb inside.

"*Danki*, Peter," she said quietly, her blue eyes warm.

He nodded and watched with satisfaction as she grasped the side of the buggy, then stepped onto the crate with her good foot. Peter remained close in the event that she wobbled and fell. But when Meg climbed into the buggy without incident, warmth and happiness flooded through him. He picked up the crate and set it on the floor in the back before getting into the front next to Meg.

"Today we'll convince Bishop John to host the party," he said with determination, "then we can continue with our plans."

Meg chuckled. "One way or another."

Meg was grateful for Peter's quick thinking in using a crate as a step for the buggy. It was as if he sensed that she wouldn't appreciate being lifted into the buggy like an invalid. If Reuben had tried to lift her, she would have been upset, but she wouldn't have said anything. After all, Reuben had saved her from drowning. She couldn't be rude to him. She owed him her life. But Peter? When he'd offered to help, she'd expected him to assist her into the buggy as he'd done when they had gone on their lunch outing with Reuben and Agnes.

She shot him a secretive glance, but looked away

before he could catch her staring. For some reason, the idea of Peter lifting her into the carriage didn't bother her the way it did with Reuben. Which made no sense, since up until recently, she and Peter hadn't gotten along.

When they arrived at Bishop John's house, Peter got out and retrieved the crate from the back of the vehicle. He gazed at her across the front seat. She smiled as he gave it to her, almost reluctantly. Meg pushed open the door and dropped the crate on the ground as Peter went around the front of the buggy to wait for her. She twisted in her seat and extended her good foot toward the crate.

"Meg," he warned, "it's not on solid ground. Hold on a second." He readjusted the wooden box so that it wouldn't shift and was closer to the buggy.

She reached down with her foot, then hesitated. If she lost her balance, she could do some serious harm to the leg while it was healing. As if sensing her thoughts, Peter held out his hand, and she accepted his help happily as she stepped off onto the ground. He released her fingers as soon as she could stand without help. Meg stifled the longing to grab his hand again as she met his gaze. *"Danki."*

He nodded then turned toward the house. "I hope he's home."

"He is," Meg said with certainty. When Peter frowned, she gestured toward the buggy parked next to the barn.

He smiled. "Sally's here."

Meg blinked. "You recognize her buggy?"

"Ja." But there was a look in his gaze that said he wasn't telling her something. He knocked and the door

immediately swung open. "*Hallo*, Sally. We've come to talk with him again."

"Come in." She stepped aside. "I just put Nicholas down for a nap."

Peter entered and then reached back for Meg's hand. She placed her fingers in his grasp, and he tugged gently to help her up the last step. Meg smiled and turned to follow his cousin. She took two steps into the house before she realized that John was sitting at the kitchen table.

"John," Peter greeted the man.

The bishop looked up. Meg thought he didn't look as tired as he'd seemed during their last visit. "You've come about the party."

Meg moved carefully as she approached. "It would mean a lot to us and our *eldre* if we could use your *haus*. You won't have to do anything. Just come." She glanced at Sally for help.

"It might be a *gut* thing," the young woman said quietly, drawing John's attention.

Was she imagining it, Meg wondered, or did John's expression soften slightly when he looked at Sally?

"It will be Christmas," Meg added. "Actually, Christmas is on church service day." She glanced toward Peter. "It would be better to have it on Second Christmas."

To her relief, Peter nodded. Second Christmas was the Amish holiday, the day after Christmas, when community members visited each other.

"John? What do you think?" she pressed. "Will you allow us to use your *haus* on Second Christmas?"

"John?" Peter said encouragingly.

John sought guidance from Sally with a look. Meg saw her nod. "*Ja*, that will be fine," the bishop replied. "You can have your birthday party here."

Meg felt a rush of warmth and relief. *"Danki."*

The man inclined his head.

"You know this is to be a surprise?" Peter said. "We want to keep my mother and Meg's father in the dark until they step inside and see everyone."

"I understand," John said, while Sally murmured in agreement.

"We should go and leave you to your day." Meg glanced about the kitchen space, gauging where the food would go.

"John, Sally," Peter said as he turned with Meg toward the door. "We appreciate it. Sally, I'll see you on Sunday."

She smiled and followed them out, watched as Meg and Peter got into the buggy, then waved.

As she glanced back, Meg saw the bishop join Sally at the door, and witnessed her quick smile for him when she realized he was there. Meg smiled in turn. She hoped that Sally and the bishop would find a new life together. They were both good people who deserved every happiness.

Meg kept her thoughts to herself as Peter drove her home. She wondered what it would be like to marry the man she loved. She frowned as she thought of Reuben Miller. She would have to make a decision about him soon, for although she was falling again for Peter Zook, and Peter was with Agnes now, it wouldn't be fair for Meg to encourage Reuben when she didn't love him. She liked him, but didn't think her feelings would ever turn into love.

Her heart fluttered as she sat next to Peter. If only she had a chance with him. She recalled the day his conversation with Josiah had revealed how he thought of her. After all these years, did he still believe her spoiled and in need of discipline? She swallowed hard. She would have to confront him and find out, though she groaned at the thought.

"Are you *oll recht*?" Peter asked with concern, and she realized he'd heard her groan.

She managed to smile, although she was feeling regret over lost time. "I'm fine," she assured him. *At least, I will be fine…eventually.*

Peter was concerned about Meg. She'd been unusually quiet since they'd left John Fisher's house, when she should be excited. They'd confirmed the party location, which was reason to celebrate. But something was clearly bothering her, and he couldn't guess what.

"Meg, we have a place to have the party," he said with a smile.

The upward curve of her lips seemed forced. He found himself wanting to grab hold of her hand, give her fingers a squeeze and ask her to tell him what was the matter. Except he had no right. She was Reuben Miller's sweetheart.

His teeth snapped together. She was Reuben's, and although he'd been trying hard to forget her and think of Agnes instead, he was having trouble getting Meg out of his mind—and out of his heart. Still, he would continue to pursue things with Agnes, because he had no choice.

Meg's house loomed ahead, and Peter took the turn. He saw another buggy in the barnyard and froze. "Meg, is that your *dat's*?" he asked, gesturing toward the other vehicle.

Meg frowned. "*Nay*, that's not ours."

Peter parked in front of the buggy. When he'd opened his door and come around to Meg's side with the wooden crate, he stiffened, seeing Reuben Miller climb out of the other vehicle.

"Reuben." Meg smiled as she carefully climbed out of the buggy without Peter's help. "I didn't expect you again today."

Peter could see the tension in Reuben's expression as he greeted the other man. "Reuben."

"Peter," he snapped in return.

"Reuben!" Meg exclaimed, clearly taken aback by his tone.

"Where have you been, Meg?"

"We had to run an errand for my father," Peter answered, before Meg could reply.

"And Meg had to ride with you?" the other man asked accusingly. "Why?"

"Because he needed my help," Meg said.

"Meg—"

"Reuben, if you're going to be rude, perhaps you should go home."

"Meg, I'm sorry."

Her face softened. "We've done nothing wrong, and I don't like that you inferred otherwise."

Peter watched the silent exchange that followed. Reuben clearly cared a great deal for Meg. Could Peter blame the man for feeling jealous? If Meg was his sweetheart, he'd have little understanding if she had come home with Reuben or any other man who wasn't family.

"I'm going to go." Peter paused and looked at Meg. "*Danki* for your help today."

She met his gaze. "You're *willkomm*, Peter." She hesitated as if she wanted to say more. "Give your *mudder* and *vadder* my best."

"I will." He turned to Reuben. "Have a nice evening, Reuben."

"Peter," the other man said, then promptly returned his attention to Meg.

As he walked around the carriage and got in, Peter couldn't help but overhear their conversation.

"Meg, I didn't mean to suggest—"

"I'm tired, Reuben. It was nice that you stopped by to see me, but I'm going upstairs to my room to take a nap. I'll see you later."

Reuben sighed. "May I come see you tomorrow?"

"I don't think so." She hesitated. "Perhaps on Friday?"

"On Friday."

Peter could hear the warmth in Reuben's voice.

Unable to stand any more of this, Peter grabbed the reins and turned his buggy toward the road. Before he pulled onto it, he turned to see that Meg and Reuben were still talking. He closed his eyes for a brief second, feeling a wave of pain. *Agnes*, he thought and turned his vehicle in the direction of the Beiler residence.

He couldn't wait for the party planning to be over. He didn't like feeling this way, caring for Meg when he knew there was no chance of having her as his sweetheart.

She might have been upset with Reuben, but Peter understood it was because of Reuben's insinuation that she'd ignored their relationship simply to spend time with him. Which Reuben would find ridiculous if he'd known the truth. But Meg couldn't tell him what was going on. She'd promised her mother, and he'd promised his father. The party would remain a secret.

As he drove toward Agnes's house, he felt the beginning of a headache. When the throbbing behind his eyes worsened, Peter decided to forget about the visit to Agnes, and he headed home instead.

As soon as the party is over, I can get on with my life...without Meg.

And that had become the most important thing—finishing and moving on without having to see Meg day in and day out, when she didn't belong to him.

Peter felt better after a good night's sleep. As he thought about his meeting with Meg, he decided that they'd spend all day together if they had to. Second Christmas was only three weeks away. The sooner they finished their plans, the better.

Meg was waiting for him by the road as he approached. She wore a black cloak over a pink dress and a matching black traveling bonnet over her prayer *kapp*. The day was chilly, and he had chosen to wear a long-sleeved shirt under his tri-blend jacket. He pulled to the side of the road and waited for her to walk the remaining few feet.

"My *vadder* and sisters are home," she gasped, out of breath.

He felt bad. Walking from her house to the street, and then to his carriage must have winded her. "What do you want to do?"

"Can we still meet? I have an idea where."

He slid over and opened the passenger-side door. He pulled out a wooden crate that he now kept in the back just for her, climbed out on her side and set it on the ground close to the buggy. He held out his hand, and she stared at it a moment before accepting his help. Peter tried not to be offended by her hesitation, but failed. Once she was settled, he ran around, stored the crate behind his seat, then climbed into the driver's seat. "Where to?" He picked up the reins and faced her.

"My *onkel* Samuel's. There is an old building in the back of the property. He doesn't use it anymore. You can access it from the road behind his farm." She stopped for a breath. "No one will know we're there."

Peter knew which road ran behind Samuel Lapp's property. He headed that direction, aware of the sudden tense silence between him and Meg as he drove.

It didn't take them long to reach the back of the property. Peter spotted the building Meg referred to, and pulled off the road to park next to it, and also behind a tree to keep the vehicle hidden.

He climbed out and eyed the old, dilapidated structure. Would they have enough light inside to see? "Meg…"

She came up next to him. "I know it's not ideal, but we can make it work. We'll find a better place next time."

Peter reached for the door, which squeaked as he swung it open. He glanced inside, saw that it was cleaner than he'd expected, and went in first to make sure it was safe for Meg. "I think this will do fine," he said, feeling better than he had upon first seeing the building.

Meg hesitated, but then ventured in. There was a scurrying sound in the corner. She gasped and backed up into him. He grabbed hold of her shoulders to keep her from falling. The scent of her shampoo and soap rose to tantalize his nose. He immediately released her. "What's wrong?"

"I heard something," she declared. "A mouse, maybe."

He bent to check every corner. "I don't see anything."

"Are you sure?" she asked, sounding nervous.

He laughed. "I'm sure. Relax, Meg. I doubt any mouse would want to stay here for long." He studied the room for something to sit on, and not finding anything, headed toward the door.

"Peter?" Meg's voice was soft, scared.

"I'll be right back," he said. "I need to get something from the buggy. Don't worry. You're safe." He saw her relax at his words. He gazed at her a long moment, admiring the blue of her eyes and the bright pink of her lips. Then he left the shed to retrieve the wooden crate. "Your chair," he said with a bow when he returned.

Meg saw the crate, and her expression warmed. "What will you sit on?"

He experienced a strange rush of pleasure that she cared. "I can sit on the ground. I'll be fine."

"Don't be silly, Peter," she objected. "We can share the crate."

He stared at the wooden box and wondered how he would be able to concentrate on the party with her sitting so close to him. He shrugged. "I'll sit when I'm tired of standing."

She gazed at him a long moment, her features unreadable, before giving a nod.

"What should we discuss first?" he asked, as she made herself comfortable on the cold wood. Peter eyed the small amount of space that she purposely left open as a seat for him. "The weather?" he said, then turned his back on her briefly as he drew a deep, silent breath. He faced her again with a smile.

"Can I talk with you about something else first?" she asked shyly.

"Certainly. What do you want to talk about?"

"I…" She briefly closed her eyes. "This is awkward."

"Go ahead. What is it?"

"Peter, do you still feel the same way about me? The way you did when I overheard you that day?"

He froze. "Meg."

"I know you considered me spoiled and in need of discipline, but do you still think that about me?"

Peter gaped at her. "Where are on earth did you get that idea?"

"I heard you, remember?"

He gazed at, his eyes widening. "I never said that about you."

"But I heard it!" she said heatedly.

He stopped, frowned and suddenly realized what she'd overheard. Then he burst out laughing. "You thought I was talking about you?" He shook his head. "I was talking about Molly! My sister's dog? Annie hadn't had her that long. She was an uncontrollable puppy when we first got her. She's a fine dog now, and my *dat* is happy to have her in the house."

Meg paled. "You were talking about a dog, and not me?"

Watching her closely, Peter gave a nod. "Not you." He sighed. "Is that what you thought?" He closed his eyes as he paced about the old wooden shed. "I never thought that about you, Meg," he said softly.

"Ach, nay," she breathed. "I…" Her voice trailed off. She seemed confused, then grew thoughtful. "Then why did you look guilty when I confronted you?"

Peter looked away.

"You had been talking about me! What did you say? What did you tell Josiah?"

He scowled. "It doesn't matter. 'Tis too late, anyway."

"Peter," she murmured, "did you like me?"

He released a sharp breath. *"Ja,"* he admitted. "I did back then."

"I'm sorry," was her only reply, which told him it wouldn't have made a difference if she had known how he felt about her.

Suddenly he'd had enough talking about the past. "Can we get back to our party planning?" he asked brusquely. "'Tis why we're here."

He saw her flinch, but couldn't do anything about it. The reminder of the day she'd yelled at him was still painful, even after all this time.

"What about if it snows?"

And just like that, they were back to business.

Chapter Thirteen

"What do you think we should do?" Meg asked hesitantly. "Have a snow date?"

Peter continued to stand. He was unwilling to sit close to her. The last thing he needed was for her to guess that he still harbored strong feelings for her. "I was thinking we could talk with your cousin Eli," he said, his voice pleasant as he tried to smooth things over. "He has a sleigh, and I know he's made one or two for other members of our community."

"That's a great idea." She seemed relaxed now that she understood what she'd heard that day, and his heart thumped hard. "We can arrange for those with sleighs to pick up those without them." She suddenly frowned. "I forgot my pencil and notes."

"I think we'll remember this. Don't you?"

"Ja." She shivered and hugged herself.

"Are you cold?" A breeze had filtered in through a crack in the wall, and he felt chilled, as well.

Meg inclined her head. "It's freezing in here."

Peter searched the room and thought about making a fire, but then quickly nixed that idea. If he tried, he was liable to burn down the old structure. He gazed at Meg, saw the look on her face and suddenly forgot his misgivings. He wanted—needed—to ensure her comfort. He moved closer, and as if understanding his intention, Meg shifted to allow him room on the stool. He sat beside her, hoping the close proximity would warm her. "I don't think it's safe to build a fire."

"Nay," she agreed, as he shifted closer to block the cold air. But he could feel her shivering. He could see their breath in the air. Her cloak wasn't keeping her warm enough.

Despite the warning his heart issued, he slipped his arm around her shoulders. He tried to ignore the fact that she felt good against him. He was there to warm her. Anyone would assist another in need, he reasoned.

"Does this help?" he asked softly. His voice sounded gravelly to his ears.

He saw her swallow. "It does. *Danki.*"

He shouldn't sit near her for long. He'd cared for her for years and was having difficulty putting aside his lingering feelings. She'd heard him talk about Molly. She hadn't heard him tell Josiah how much he loved her. Now that she knew about the dog, he didn't want her to suspect how deep his feelings for her had been—and still were. Peter knew he took a terrible risk by sitting next to her now.

"What else do we have to discuss?" He knew he should remove his arm. Instead, he kept it where it was, but shifted away slightly. He stifled a groan when Meg followed him as he moved; she clearly enjoyed the warmth he provided.

"We'll have to ask my *mam* and your *dat* about who to invite. If we're going to keep it a surprise, we'll have to be careful to ensure the gathering stays relatively small. Otherwise word will get out." She placed her hands in her lap.

She seemed to be feeling warmer, he thought with a sense of satisfaction. "I agree. Can you think of anything else?" He needed to put distance between them. This situation wasn't easy for him. He conjured up thoughts of Agnes—her blond hair…her bright expression…her smile—but Meg's image kept superimposing itself over Agnes's features. He scowled and shifted farther away.

A long moment of silence ensued. Peter caught her staring at him. Awareness sprang up between them, shocking him with its intensity. She looked startled, so he knew she felt it, too. With a sound of regret, he stood. "We should leave." He walked away, desperate to escape her.

He knew the exact moment she stood. He stiffened as he heard her approach from behind. "Peter," she murmured. There was an odd little catch in her voice.

He felt off balance when she touched his shoulder. He spun out of instinct. A tremor of feeling overwhelmed and angered him. "What are you doing, Meg?" he growled. "I'm with Agnes." And he didn't have to add, "And you're with Reuben."

She retreated as if stung. Her mouth worked, like she wanted to say something but didn't know how to respond. To his dismay, he watched as tears filled her blue eyes. He felt a tightening in his belly. Regret overwhelmed him, but he kept silent.

"I think you should take me home," she whispered brokenly.

Unable to look away, he held her hurt-filled gaze. He felt the urge to hold and comfort her, but fought to ignore it. Instead he nodded and picked up the crate. She hurried outside, seemingly unmindful of her leg brace. Peter followed quickly, and when Meg stumbled, he reached out to steady her. She immediately jerked away, then continued slowly to the passenger side of the buggy, as though taking extra care to ensure she wouldn't have to endure his touch again. When she reached the vehicle, she eyed the step and froze. He knew she was upset that she couldn't climb in without help.

Without a word, Peter set the crate down for her, then stepped back. He had wounded her, and it hadn't been his intention. When she hurt, he did, too. But he could take only so much while trying to get over his feelings for a woman who confused and confounded him.

It took two tries before Meg was successfully situated in the front seat. Without a word, he picked up the crate, went around to his side and set it behind him before he slid in next to her. He swiveled in his seat to face her, but she stared ahead, unwilling to meet his gaze.

"Meg." She stiffened. "Are we going to be able to work together?"

She faced him briefly, her eyes bright, her expression cold, before she averted her gaze. *"Ja."*

He picked up the leathers and focused on the road ahead. He'd known it had been a mistake to sit next to her. It had been a terrible error on his part to think that he could be alone with her in an abandoned building. What were they going to do the next time they needed a private place to plan the party?

He drove in silence. Meg didn't say a word until he pulled into her yard and came around the vehicle with the crate.

She stepped down. "Bye, Peter." And with that, she promptly started toward the house.

"Meg!"

Her shoulders tensed as she halted, then turned. *"Ja?"*

He was filled with regret, gazing at her. "I'm sorry," he said. "I didn't mean to upset you." His anger was actually directed at himself. "I feel as though we've become friends. Are you still willing to work with me? We have a lot to do."

It seemed, for a moment, that she would refuse. "We can talk about it on Sunday."

Visiting Sunday was just days away. He released a pent-up breath as Meg entered the house. Considering their past history, there would be some explaining to do if anyone other than her mother discovered that he and Meg had spent time together.

Meg blinked back tears as she watched from inside the house as Peter left. What had happened to set him off? Their morning had started out well. He'd been kind, and it seemed as if today they would accomplish a lot. Then he'd thought of her comfort when she'd been chilled by the cold breeze in the shed. He'd sat close to warm her, and it had felt right. Especially after she'd confronted him and finally learned the truth about the past—that he and Josiah had been discussing Molly, the dog, not her. And when she realized that they had discussed her as well, she'd wanted to know what they'd said. The strange look on his face had simply made her wonder, and so she'd asked. To learn that he had liked her was both a vindication and a curse, because it was too late to do anything about it now that Peter had Agnes in his life.

After they'd talked a bit about the party, the next thing she knew Peter was suddenly bolting out of his seat, clearly upset for some reason—over what, she had no idea. She'd gotten up to comfort him, to see if she could help. And he'd turned on her.

He'd become angry. Why? He'd all but accused her of stealing him away from Agnes! She wouldn't do that. *As if I could.* She cared for Peter. That he had the power to hurt her told her just how much. And because she did, she wanted him to be happy. Even if his happiness hinged on being with Agnes Beiler.

Meg headed toward the back of the house. *"Mam?"* There was no answer. She tried again. She prayed that no one other than her mother was at home. The last thing she needed was for any of her sisters to realize she'd been with Peter.

She heard footsteps on the stairs. She turned back as Ellie descended from the second floor.

"Meg?" Ellie looked concerned at first, then relieved at seeing her. "Where have you been?"

"I had an errand to run and got a ride."

Her sister narrowed her gaze but didn't pursue the conversation, and for that Meg was grateful.

"What are you doing home?" Meg asked. "I thought you had a house to clean."

Ellie made a face. "I did, but on my way over, my client called and canceled on me."

"I'm sorry," she said, and started toward the kitchen.

"Meg, are you crying?"

She shook her head.

"But you were," Ellie pressed.

"I'm fine. It's cold out." She glanced back and smiled to ease her sibling's concern. "Just hungry."

Ellie grinned. "Let's eat then. What would you like? I'll cook."

"I think *Mam* already made lunch." Meg frowned.

"Where is she? She was next door earlier. She can't still be there."

"She's meeting *Dat* in town." Ellie smirked. "They're eating out."

Meg felt a jolt of surprise. "That's nice."

Her heart gave a lurch as she thought of Peter. He was constantly in her thoughts.

She helped Ellie by setting the table while her sister pulled out the pot of soup her mother had made earlier that morning. When they finally sat down together, Meg looked at Ellie. "Do you know where we're going for visiting day?"

"I believe the Zooks have invited us for this Sunday."

Meg suddenly lost her appetite. They'd be going to Peter's house. She knew she'd have to talk with him, to decide when they would meet next, for she knew that she wouldn't be able to stop working with him. Despite the fact that he apparently liked Agnes enough to have her as his sweetheart, Meg realized that she still wanted—needed—to spend time with him. Planning the party would be the only time she'd have with him. Once the party was over, they'd go their separate ways. She'd still see him at church services and occasionally on visiting day, but it wouldn't be the same. They'd say *hallo*, then spend the rest of their time apart.

She experienced a burning in her chest. He'd hurt her, made her feel as if she'd done something wrong, but except for this morning, she couldn't regret her time with him. If only she hadn't overheard him that day years ago. If only she hadn't yelled at him.

And Reuben. She needed to have a conversation with Reuben. She couldn't go on allowing him to think she was serious about him when she wasn't. Maybe someday she'd find a man to love and marry, but it wouldn't be anytime soon. Not while her heart still longed for Peter.

The next morning Meg helped her mother and sisters make food to bring to the Joseph Zook homestead. Then on Sunday morning, she got into the buggy with her parents and her sisters Leah, Ellie and Charlie, who still lived at home. She had almost asked to stay back, but then realized that would only upset her family.

Meg closed her eyes and prayed that today would go better than the last day she'd spent time with Peter Zook.

When they arrived, Peter was outside with her cousin Jacob. He glanced her way as she got out of the buggy with her father's help. She thought she saw his lips curve in a half smile as her *dat* released her arm.

The last thing she expected was for Peter to break away from Jacob and approach her.

"Arlin," he said in greeting. "Missy. May I have a quick word with Meg?"

Her father looked surprised, but nodded. "We'll be inside, *dochter*," he said.

Meg swallowed as she watched her parents leave her. Ellie lingered until Meg shot her a warning glance. Leah waved for Charlie and Ellie to follow. Meg felt her tension grow as her family disappeared into the house, leaving her alone with Peter.

"Meg."

She met his gaze. "Peter."

"I'm sorry." There was genuine sorrow in his expression, and it moved her. "I can't explain, but please know that it wasn't my intention to hurt you."

She couldn't look away. His gray eyes had darkened to almost black. There was an earnestness in them that touched her heart and encouraged her to forgive him.

And it was easy to forgive him, she realized. She loved him, although she'd make sure that he never knew.

She became lost in his focused attention. "Apology accepted."

Relief softened his features. "So you'll still work with me on the party?"

She nodded. "When—and where—would you like to meet?"

He appeared to give it some thought. "Tuesday? I have to handle some business for my *vadder* tomorrow."

"Tuesday will be fine. Where?"

A flicker of relief moved across his face. "I can come get you, and we'll go to Ephrata for lunch. No one will see us there."

"But where should I say I'm going?"

"I'm sure your *mudder* will help with that. Just explain to her that it will be difficult to keep the party a surprise if any of our family members see us together."

Peter observed the changing expressions on Meg's face. Going all the way to Ephrata was the best plan, but before he went with Meg, he needed to pay a visit to Agnes. It had been days since he'd seen her, and while previously she'd been distracted by her cousins' visit, he suspected that her relatives had been long gone. He had working in the shop as an excuse for some of that time. But some of it he'd spent with Meg. And if she found out, Agnes would never understand.

"You don't have to pick me up. We can meet at Whittier's Store if it will help?"

"*Nay*, everyone we know and his *bruder* shops at that store. We're bound to see someone if we meet there. I don't think that's wise." Peter thought a minute. "When do you go back to the doctor? Maybe I can take you."

Her eyes brightened. "That would work." Her expression dimmed. "But I'm not due to see the doctor for another two weeks."

Peter grinned. "But do your sisters and father know that?"

"I'm not sure. I doubt it." A slow smile settled on her pink mouth. "I'll see what *Mam* says." She glanced toward the house. "We should go or they will think something is up."

"And it is," he said. "But you're right." He paused. "Tell your *mam* your appointment should be at eleven." When she looked at him in question, he explained, "We'll eat lunch while we plan."

She agreed. "What should I say if anyone asks why you wanted to speak with me?"

"Tell them I was concerned about your leg and wanted to know how you were managing."

She eyed him carefully. "And are you concerned? About my leg?" she added, after a brief hesitation.

"*Ja*, I'm concerned about your leg." *I'm concerned about you.* Which was why he stayed close, ready to help her in case she fell. And why he'd used the crate to help her get into his buggy.

A softness entered her blue eyes, warming him, making him wish for things that could never be. She blinked, and he pulled himself together. He headed toward the house with her by his side, and the rightness of the moment hit him hard.

He sighed. It was just an illusion—he and Meg together.

To his surprise, she allowed him to assist her into the house. People were scattered throughout his home, some in the living room, others in the kitchen. To his relief, no one looked at him strangely when he and Meg entered together. Except Meg's sister Ellie. Peter smiled at her and gestured toward Meg's leg brace. As if she understood, Ellie nodded and returned his smile before she continued her conversation with Annie.

Meg took off her coat, then went in one direction while he left for the opposite side of the room. But as he joined his father and the group of men who decided they should head to the barn this fine blustery cold day, Peter found his thoughts still with Meg, who stayed inside with the women.

Suddenly, despite himself, he discovered he was looking forward to their next party-planning meeting on Tuesday in Ephrata.

Chapter Fourteen

It was freezing in the barn. Peter stood by his father and listened as he talked about spring crops and their horses in the stable. Peter thought they'd be better off in the forge, where they could light a fire and stay warm, but the others—Samuel Lapp and five of his seven sons, Abram Peachy and his three sons, and Arlin Stoltzfus—didn't seem affected by the cold. Peter wore a long-sleeved shirt under his black woolen jacket, but still he shivered.

As he wrapped his arms around himself, he thought of Meg and how cold she'd been in Samuel Lapp's old outbuilding—and the way he'd tried to warm her. Those few moments seated close to her had felt wonderful and right, until he'd realized the direction of his thoughts and known he'd have to keep fighting the way he felt about her. Before he did something he couldn't take back. Like profess his love for her. Which would be an awful mistake, since Reuben was her sweetheart now. Except for their recent working relationship, Meg had never given him any attention, except when forced and then she'd seemed annoyed.

His ears were like ice. He readjusted his woolen hat.

It was ridiculous to stand out here when there was perfectly good heat in the house.

"I'm considering planting potatoes this spring," his father said.

"Potatoes?" Peter stared at him with disbelief. "I like potatoes, *Dat*, but we may need to look into it first." He shifted uncomfortably when the men turned their gazes on him. "You plan to sell them?"

Horseshoe Joe shrugged. "Just thinking about it. Not sure if it will be potatoes or corn." Was his *dat* angered or pleased by Peter's concern?

"You can't feed potatoes to your livestock, Joe," Noah Lapp pointed out.

"True." He eyed Peter with a strange look.

Tension followed in the ensuing silence. Peter decided it was a signal for him to leave. He and his father could talk about potatoes later, after everyone had gone home. "I'm going back to the house. I could use a cup of hot coffee." He headed for the barn door.

"Me, too," Noah Lapp said. His wife, Rachel, was inside with their two children, Katherine and four-month-old Luke.

Peter paused to wait for Meg's cousin, then the two of them hurried out of the barn and toward the house.

"I don't know what it is about our *vadders*," Noah said. "I'm a *dat* now, and I can't see the sense in standing in the cold, freezing my toes off."

He laughed. "Yet there we were, following them as if we had to." Peter regarded him with a grin. "But we came to our senses."

"*Ja*, praise the Lord."

A buggy pulled onto the lane, drawing Peter's attention. "I wonder who that is."

Noah narrowed his eyes. "Can't tell, but it looks like there are two women inside."

"Agnes," Peter decided, as he took a closer look. And Alice.

"Who's Agnes?" Noah asked. Peter hadn't realized he'd spoken aloud.

"A friend."

Meg's cousin arched one eyebrow. "A close one?"

"Not yet."

"Given up on Meg, have you?"

Peter sighed as he met the other man's gaze. "Trying to."

"I see." Noah's warm eyes held understanding.

The buggy pulled off onto the grass and stopped. Agnes hopped out on the driver's side while her sister got out of the vehicle more slowly. After a quick glance at Noah, Peter veered toward the girls.

"Surprise!" Agnes exclaimed with a grin.

Peter smiled. He couldn't help himself. How could he with Agnes beaming at him? He realized that Noah had approached, too. Apparently, the man was willing to brave the cold long enough to satisfy his curiosity.

"A nice surprise," Peter said. "*Hallo*, Agnes. Alice." The girls' gazes settled on Noah.

"This is Noah Lapp." He saw something flicker in Agnes's gaze. "Noah, meet Agnes and her sister Alice."

"Twins," Noah murmured. "And identical. I have twin brothers, but they look nothing alike." His lips curved upward. "We were just headed inside. It must be zero degrees out here."

"There's a thermometer on the porch," Peter said. He addressed the sisters. "Want to get warm?"

Agnes nodded and fell into step with him. "I know I took a chance coming here without being invited."

"You don't need an invitation, Agnes." He waited for her to precede him up the steps. Behind them, Alice chatted with Noah.

"I wasn't sure." Agnes met his gaze. "I haven't seen you for a while."

Peter felt his stomach muscles clench. "*Ja*, you had company and I had to help my *dat* in the shop."

"You could have come over while my cousins were still here."

"I know," he admitted, "and I'm sorry."

She accepted his apology with warmth. "'Tis *oll recht*." Her gaze roamed over him, making him uneasy.

As he held the door open for Agnes and Alice, with Noah following them into the house, Peter thought of Meg. How would she react to seeing Agnes again? Especially after the way he'd brought up her name in the shed. Perhaps a bigger question was how *he* was reacting to seeing Agnes, after he'd given in to his feelings for Meg, the ones he'd been forever struggling to forget?

Meg came out of the kitchen as he and Agnes headed that way. "Agnes," she said with a smile. "I didn't know you were here."

He caught an odd look in Agnes's eyes as she smiled back. "Meg, you're looking well." She took in Meg's leg brace. "You've gotten your cast off." She seemed genuinely pleased for her.

"*Ja*, thanks be to *Gott*. The cast was cumbersome. With this, I can walk without crutches."

Peter met Meg's gaze over the top of Agnes's head. Their eyes held, and he felt something transpire between them before he averted his glance. Agnes stepped back to allow him to move up from behind her.

"We've come in to warm up. Any coffee or tea on?" he asked.

Something altered in Meg's expression, but it was gone so fast, he thought he'd imagined it. "*Ja*, both." She smiled again. "I've come to visit with Rachel. I haven't had a chance to hold Luke yet."

"Luke is Noah's infant son," Peter explained.

Their attention shifted to where Noah stood beside his wife, smiling down at her. As he watched, Peter saw Noah reach out to run a finger gently over his son's baby-soft skin. The sight filled Peter with yearning. He'd like to have children of his own. He turned back—and locked gazes with Meg.

"I'd better move, before Rachel decides to put Luke down for a nap upstairs and I lose this opportunity." Meg walked carefully to the couple and their children. Katherine sat at her mother's feet, playing with a doll. As with all their children's dolls, Katherine's had no face, but she wore a black bonnet and blue dress with a black apron.

"Noah seems happy," Agnes commented, drawing Peter's gaze.

He smiled. "He is. I've not seen a happier man since he fell in love and married Rachel."

Agnes peered up at him with an intensity that made the hairs at the back of his neck rise. "How did they meet?" She reined back her look, and he relaxed.

"Rachel is Amos King's niece. She came to Happiness to be our new schoolteacher." He studied Noah's wife with warmth that turned to concern as he thought of everything Rachel had suffered in the past. "She was in a terrible buggy accident several months before she came here. Happiness was a new start for her. But she wasn't our schoolteacher for long. Noah swept her off her feet and they wed. It doesn't appear she regrets her choice of husband."

"*Nay*," Agnes agreed softly.

Something in her tone troubled him, but he still managed to grin. "Ready for something hot to drink?" She nodded. "Coffee or tea?"

"Either one is fine." She followed him into the kitchen. "Unless you have the fixings for hot chocolate."

Peter faced her. "I believe I do." He greeted his mother and introduced Agnes to the women who hadn't met her previously. "*Mam*, I'm going to make us some hot cocoa."

Miriam Zook smiled. "Help yourself."

While he heated milk in a saucepan, Peter listened as Agnes chatted with his mother and his aunt Alta Hershberger. Alta, his cousin Sally's mother, would natter about Agnes and him the first opportunity she got. Unfortunately for her, many of their friends were here and had already seen them together, which would bother his dear aunt to no end, to have no fresh gossip.

"Anyone else want a cup of hot chocolate?" Peter asked, as the milk heated and started to steam.

"Nay," his mother said, echoed by the other women.

He added cocoa powder to the hot milk, then sweetened it with sugar and a touch of vanilla. "Would you like to sit here? Or in the other room?" Peter asked, a cup of hot chocolate in each hand.

"Alice is in the other room," Agnes said.

"Other room it is." He flashed the women a grin. "If you see another one like her, it's her twin sister, Alice."

"We've seen them both before," Alta informed him with a sniff. "They came to church services and once to visiting Sunday in the past."

Peter nodded. *"Ja*, they did," he said patiently. He turned to Agnes. "We can sit at that table."

He set the mugs on the table near the window and pulled up a wooden chair for Agnes. Alice was on the other side of the room talking with Isaac, Daniel and Joseph Lapp. She caught Agnes's glance and waved with a smile, but didn't approach.

"How is it?" Peter asked, as Agnes picked up her mug and took a sip.

"Delicious."

"I'm a man of many talents."

She arched an eyebrow. "Are you? What else can you do?"

"I can shoe a horse and farm a field, and I can make a pot of coffee when I want to."

Agnes's gaze intensified. "You are talented indeed. I don't know of a single man who would do more than those first two things. But you can make hot cocoa and a pot of coffee. Impressive."

"'Tis nothing," he murmured. Laughter drew his gaze. It was Meg, seated in the chair that Rachel had vacated, with little Luke in her lap. She was nose to nose with him. When the baby cooed, Meg's pleasure rippled out with a joyful chuckle.

"He's adorable, Rachel," Meg said with a grin.

"We think so," Noah agreed. "Takes after his father."

Rachel snorted. "Does he now?"

Noah gazed at his wife with adoration. "You know he does. You told me yourself only this morning." He glanced down at his son. "When he was sleeping like the sweet boy he is."

Peter saw Rachel put her hand on Noah's arm. Most husbands and wives in their world didn't display their affection around others, but Peter could see the love Rachel and Noah had for each other in a simple touch, a quick smile.

"I'd like one of those," Agnes commented softly.

"Those?" He met her gaze.

"A baby." Her face filled with longing as she studied the child from across the room. When her attention returned to him, Agnes looked hopeful.

Peter suffered a momentary discomfort. He'd felt the pressure to marry because of his parents. And Agnes would make a good wife. He wanted a future with her, didn't he? Then why couldn't he see himself married to Agnes, or visualize the child they might have? The only images in his mind that seemed real were of a little girl with dark hair and blue eyes—and of Meg as his bride and his child's mother.

He experienced a tight feeling in his chest. Lord help him. He was still desperately in love with Meg Stoltzfus.

Meg could feel Peter's gaze on her as she played with little Luke. She didn't look in his direction. He had studied her earlier, with an odd glimmer in his eyes. She hadn't known what to make of it at the time.

She cooed to the baby, and Luke cooed back. She laughed and looked up to see a smile on Rachel's face, and an expression of happiness on Noah's. She met the boy's gaze again and could tell that Luke was getting tired. "Rachel? I have a feeling your son is about to become upset." As if on cue, the baby scrunched up his little features and let out a whimper, then a wail.

Meg handed the child to his mother and rose awkwardly to her feet. Her brace made getting up and down a little difficult, but it was much better than the cast she'd worn previously. "And this is my cue to leave." She murmured to Noah, "*Ja*, Noah, you're right." When he frowned, she teased, "He takes after his father."

She caught his grin before she turned. Her gaze collided with Peter's. She felt the impact of meeting his eyes in the tingle at her nape and the hot flush of her cheeks. Eager to escape, she started toward the kitchen.

"Meg." Agnes appeared at her elbow. The young woman held a mug and walked with her. "How's Reuben?"

Meg sensed Peter's presence as he approached from behind. The air went still. She hadn't seen Reuben for a while, but she didn't want Agnes—or Peter—to know that. After a heartbeat, she said, "He's fine. He's completely healed after the accident. Like me, the bruises on his face have disappeared."

"But you still wear a brace," Agnes commiserated.

She didn't know why, but something in the girl's tone got her back up. She reined in her impatience and smiled. "The doctor said the bone's healing nicely. I may get rid of this thing early."

"How nice."

Meg couldn't tell if Agnes's smile was genuine. She wanted to leave. She didn't feel like having idle chitchat with Peter's sweetheart. "I think I'll head outside for a breath of air." She moved toward the front of the house, grabbed her coat from a hook near the door, slipped it on, then ventured outside.

The air was frigid, and Meg saw her breath wisp out as visible steam. Her heart beat hard within her chest. She closed her eyes and tried to forget the sight of Peter and Agnes seated side by side, drinking hot chocolate as if they'd done it together many times.

The fact that she hadn't seen Reuben should bother her, but it didn't. And that alone told her it was past time for her to break it off with him. *The next time I see him, I will.*

The door behind her opened, and she stiffened. Surely Agnes hadn't decided to join her outside. She turned and saw with relief that it was her sister Charlie. "Hey."

Charlie joined her at the porch railing. "'Tis quiet out here. Too crowded in there," she said.

Meg shrugged. "I didn't think so." Until Agnes and her sister had shown up. Then the house had seemed too full with their presence—and Agnes's role in Peter's life.

"I wish we could go home."

Something in her little sister's tone alerted her. Meg faced her and touched her arm. "What's wrong, Charlotte?"

Charlie twisted her lips at being addressed by her given name. She'd always used her nickname since they'd moved to Happiness, especially since Abram Peachy's wife was also named Charlotte. "I didn't know the Peachys would be here," her sister complained.

"They're *gut* people. Why are you upset?"

"Nathaniel Peachy." Charlie's features contorted with disgust. "I don't like him."

"Nate," Meg mused. "He giving you a hard time, little *schweschter*?" Her sister nodded. "Want me to go and take him down a peg or two? Give him a severe talking-to for treating you poorly?"

Charlie appeared horrified by Meg's offer. "*Nay*, don't you dare!" She hugged herself tightly. "You'll give him a swollen head, making him think he has the power to annoy me. Better to ignore him."

Meg nodded with approval. "You're learning, *maydel*." She grinned. "You've made me happy to be your big sister."

The door behind them opened again, and the object of her sister's frustration exited the house. Meg watched as Charlie studied the man, who swept by them with a murmur, hurrying toward his family's buggy. The sound of the door opening again had Meg turning. She'd expected to see the rest of the Peachy family, but it was Peter and the Beiler twins. Peter's gaze glanced off her as he accompanied the sisters toward their parked vehicle.

"Have a nice day, Meg," Agnes said, as she continued past. Her arm brushed against Peter's, she hovered so close. "Take care of that leg."

"I will, Agnes." Meg felt her teeth snap together as she watched Agnes deliberately bump against Peter several times. "I wonder if *Dat* and *Mam* are ready to leave yet," she said to her sister when they were out of earshot.

Charlie sighed. "I doubt it. We haven't eaten yet."

Meg knew she was right. They would have to stay for the midday meal, but as soon as she could, she would suggest they head home. She'd plead exhaustion if she had to, for she was tired from having to endure the sight of Peter with Agnes.

Her sister turned back to the house and Meg followed. She wasn't hungry. Her appetite had vanished the instant Agnes had walked in.

A man she didn't love wanted her, while she yearned for someone who didn't care for her, a man she didn't have a hope of having for her own. Meg sighed. She wanted nothing more than to go home, crawl into bed and sleep to forget the heartache she was destined to suffer in the weeks ahead. For things in her life would certainly change between now and the party. She'd no longer have Reuben in her life, and would no longer get to work with the man she loved—a man who wanted another.

Chapter Fifteen

As she came out of the house, Meg looked perturbed, Peter noted. He was waiting for her at the bottom of the steps for their day in Ephrata.

"What's wrong?" he asked with a frown.

"Remember that great idea we had that my *mam* could tell my family you'd be taking me to the doctor? We thought it a *gut* excuse for us to be in each other's company."

"Ja." Peter studied her with concern. Her expression was sheepish. "How bad can it be? Just tell me."

"Mam made sure she'd be telling the truth when she told my *dat* and sisters." She paused, looking upset. "I have a doctor's appointment today at eleven." She met his gaze as if begging for understanding. "In thirty minutes."

"Is that all?" he asked. Peter was relieved. He thought something terrible had happened. "That's not a problem. I'll take you to your doctor's appointment, then we can go to Ephrata for lunch when you're done."

Meg blinked. "Are you sure? You knew nothing about this—"

"Meg, I did offer to take you to your doctor's and physical therapy appointments."

Her face cleared. "*Ja*, you did."

"Then let's go, shall we?" He offered her his arm, because it felt like the right thing to do.

She didn't hesitate this time, but grabbed hold and allowed him to help her down the few steps and then into the carriage. "I don't know why she made this appointment. I didn't think I was due for one until another week at least."

"Did your *mudder* talk with the doctor the last time you were there?"

"*Ja.*" Meg sighed. "Maybe he told her something he didn't tell me?"

"Could be. Maybe he thinks you're healing well enough that you can start physical therapy sooner than expected, and he didn't want to get your hopes up until he could x-ray your leg and know for sure."

Her blue eyes brightened as she turned in her seat to meet his gaze while he climbed into the buggy. "Do you think so?"

"I guess we'll find out." There was a nip in the air, but Peter barely noticed it. He was feeling warm inside with Meg beside him. He was glad they'd mended their working relationship. Now that she knew the truth about what she'd overheard, Meg seemed more willing to be friends. They hadn't yet reached the depth of friendship that he shared with Agnes, but it meant a lot to him. Considering how he'd felt about her for so long, it was a big deal to him.

They made it to the doctor's office and had Meg checked in within twenty minutes of leaving her house. As he sat beside her in the waiting room after hanging up their coats, Peter studied her leg brace and hoped he was right, and she was ready for physical therapy. She looked pretty in a purple dress that did wonderful things to her dark hair and blue eyes.

"Did you bring your invitation list?" Meg asked, drawing his attention from her leg to her face.

He nodded. "When I asked, *Dat* had a list ready. As if he was expecting me to ask."

"My *mam* did, too."

A nurse called Meg's name. Peter helped her to rise, then watched as she made her way across the room to the door where the woman waited. "Sir," the nurse said, "you may come in with your wife."

Peter experienced a jolt. "I…"

Meg met his gaze, and to his surprise, he saw her lips curve with amusement. "That's all right. My husband is a bit squeamish. He can wait here."

The nurse nodded as if she understood, and Meg disappeared into a back room.

The minutes went by, and it seemed as if Meg was gone a long time. Peter began to worry. Was she all right? Had the doctor discovered a problem with her leg? Maybe it hadn't healed as well as he'd first thought.

The door to the back area opened. "Peter?" the nurse called. "Meg would like you to come on back."

Peter rose as the shock of Meg's request had his heart thumping hard, ready to burst out of his chest. If only he were Meg's husband, with the right to be there for her as he'd longed for since he'd first set eyes on her and fallen in love. His legs trembled as he approached, until reason gave him pause and the strength to continue on. Meg wanted him in the exam room with her. Either she had received terrible news and needed his support, or she had learned something *gut* enough to want to share the moment.

"Here you are. She's in room two, waiting for you."

Peter swallowed hard before he entered. The doctor was typing into a computer on a tiny table that extended from a countertop. Meg sat in a chair close to the exam table, and immediately locked gazes with Peter. Concern filled him. He wanted to comfort her if the news was bad, and hug her if the news was good. Her expression unreadable, she stared at him a long moment, then gestured toward the next seat.

The doctor finished typing, then looked up. "*Hallo.* You must be Peter." He turned to Meg. "I looked at the X-rays from your last visit, Meg, and compared them to those." He indicated the light on the wall that lit up a set of films. "I have to say that I'm surprised by the change."

Peter felt Meg shift. "Is it a good change or bad?" she asked, as she reached to grab Peter's hand.

The physician smiled. "Good change. Meg, your leg is healed. I can't believe it myself. You must have amazing recuperative powers because your leg is healed enough for you to begin physical therapy. Normally it takes six to eight weeks for a broken bone to mend. Sometimes longer, but you… Your leg has repaired itself in just under five weeks from your accident."

Peter flashed her a smile as he squeezed her fingers gently. He expected her to pull her hand away, but she didn't. Instead, she held on and squeezed back.

"I didn't always have amazing healing ability," Meg murmured.

"*Ja*, you have, Meg," Peter assured her. She had come through a serious illness where her life could have been cut short at age fourteen.

She held his gaze, seemed to glean his thoughts. She faced the doctor. "I can start physical therapy?"

"Yes," the doctor said. "But you need to continue to wear the brace as much as possible. You may take it off for short periods, though. That'll be a nice change, won't it?"

Meg grinned. "Yes."

"Where should she go for therapy?" Peter asked, as if he were her husband and had the right to know.

Dr. Reckling mentioned a facility that was close enough to make it easy for both Meg and him as the driver.

As they left the office shortly afterward, Meg stood on the sidewalk and drew in a deep breath. "That was worth the trip," she said quietly.

Peter's lips curved upward. "*Ja*, it was." He had the urge to hug her. They gazed at each other a long moment, and he gave in to the feeling. He moved close, reached out and pulled her into his arms for a hug. He made it quick so it didn't feel awkward for either of them, but he felt a rush of satisfaction that he had the chance to hold her in his arms, however briefly.

Meg's face was red as he stepped back. He pretended not to notice. "Let's go eat," he said. "We've got a party to finish planning."

They ate lunch in a diner nearby and looked over each other's invitation lists. "They're the same," Meg said with raised eyebrows.

Peter chuckled. "As if our parents created it together."

"They probably did, when they decided they wanted the birthday party."

"Well, that simplifies things," Peter said as he pulled out cash for the check. When Meg opened her mouth as if she would object, he held up his hand. "I asked you to lunch, Meg."

Her lips firmed, but she didn't say another word, as if she knew she couldn't win the argument.

As they drove back to Happiness, they talked about the party food, knowing that the women who were to be invited would want to contribute.

Meg convinced him to allow others to fix food. "I'd want to bring my share if I was invited to a party or gathering."

The list included family of the birthday pair and a number of their closest friends. Not too many, though, that they couldn't invite them personally, starting the next day.

At her house, Peter came around the buggy to help her up her porch steps. "Don't want to do anything to postpone your physical therapy," he said with a little smirk.

The door opened as they reached the landing. Missy Stoltzfus stood in the opening, as if waiting for them.

"Mam," Meg cried with excitement. "My leg's healed. Dr. Reckling wants me to wear the brace for a while longer, but I can start physical therapy, and I don't have to wear it all the time."

Her mother was delighted. "Peter," she said, *"danki* for taking her."

"I was happy to help." He hesitated. "I'd be glad to take Meg to her physical therapy appointments if you don't mind." He kept his eyes focused on Meg's mother.

Missy nodded. "That would be wonderful. She'll have to go often, and while her father or I can take her to some of them, we'd really appreciate your help."

"Gut," Peter said. "Then it's all set. Her first therapy session is on Monday. I'll take her then." He met Missy's gaze. "We can talk about last-minute party arrangements."

"An excellent idea. In fact, you can take her to all her appointments next week if you have the time."

"I should," he said. "If for some reason I can't, I'll let you know." He turned to Meg. "I'll come by for you tomorrow."

She nodded. When she caught her mother's questioning look, Meg said, "We thought we'd invite those on your list personally."

Her *mam* eyed them with approval. "If someone asks why you're here again, Peter, I'll explain that you're taking Meg to see where she'll be having her therapy before she starts next week."

"We'll find the office," Peter said. His gaze settled gently on Meg. "We got a lot done today. Just over two weeks, and the party will have come and gone." And the thought, he realized, saddened him. "I should get home and check in with *Dat* and Jacob in the shop. I'll see you tomorrow, Meg. Missy."

He left, thinking of Meg and how happy she was about her leg. He was glad he'd be the one taking her to PT some of the time, if not all. Peter suddenly thought of Reuben Miller, and the joy in his day with Meg dissipated. He had to stay committed to Agnes. In fact, he'd stop in briefly to see her before he headed home.

He made a turn that took him onto the road that led to the Joshua Beiler farm and Agnes. He attempted to see the bright side. Agnes's disposition could brighten anyone's day. If anyone could help him fight his feelings for Meg, it would be Agnes.

Then why couldn't he forget the way Meg had held on to his hand in the doctor's office?

Agnes, he thought. *Think of Agnes.* And so he did… until he reached her house and learned that she wasn't there. He went home then, his thoughts veering from Meg to Agnes, then back to Meg. *Nay!*

But Meg's smiling face haunted him. No matter how hard he tried, he couldn't get her out of his mind.

Meg rose early with a grin on her face. She was ready for her day. Peter would be coming for her at ten. She sat up, swung her legs off the bed and reached for her brace. It took a moment's struggle, but she was able to slip it on. She rose carefully, stood a moment until her body settled and she felt stable.

When she was ready, she went downstairs to breakfast. She had reached the bottom of the steps when she heard her mother call out to her.

"Ja, Mam?"

"Come into the kitchen. You have a visitor!"

Peter. Her heart thumped. "Coming!" The man turned as she entered the kitchen. "Reuben!" She experienced a vague disappointment. "You're here."

He smiled. "I had to work a lot these last two weeks, Meg. Sorry I couldn't stop by before now."

She moved to sit in her chair. "I was just going to have something to eat. Want to join me?"

Reuben shook his head. He had taken off his hat, and his blond hair was thick and shiny. The sun pouring through the window glistened on the golden strands. "I can't stay, Meg. I wanted to see you before I went to the construction site."

"You still have to work?" She was actually glad he'd be gone before Peter's arrival. It would have been awkward for the two of them to meet up again, given the fact that there was something about Peter that Reuben didn't like. And vice versa.

"I'm sorry, Meg." His blue eyes shone with regret.

"I understand," she assured him. "Maybe you can stop by again, tomorrow after work? I'd like to talk with you. Will you come?" She paused. "If you don't have to work too late."

Reuben smiled. "*Ja*, I'll come tomorrow after work." He stood, picked up his hat. "You look well, Meg. Missy told me that your leg has healed nicely and you'll be starting physical therapy next week."

"*Ja.*" She eyed him carefully. "Your bruises are gone, and you are back to work, so I imagine you're feeling your former self."

"The only soreness I feel now is from a full day's work." He started for the door, where he paused. "I'll see you tomorrow."

He left, and Meg reached across the table for the plate of muffins. "It was nice of Reuben to visit," she commented to her mother.

"You didn't expect him to come?"

Meg took a bite of a chocolate muffin and shook her head. "*Nay*, it's been a while since I saw him last." She met her mother's gaze. "He was out of town, visiting family, and then he had to work," she explained.

"Would you like me to invite him to supper tomorrow night?" her mother asked.

Shaking her head, Meg said, "*Nay*, I don't know that he'll want to stay after I talk with him."

Mam widened her eyes. "Ah, so that's the way of it then."

"*Ja*, I'm afraid so."

"Better now than later."

Meg hoped that Reuben felt the same after she broke up with him, although the truth was she'd never consented to his courtship of her in the first place.

"*Hallo!* Anybody home? Meg?"

Meg heard Peter's voice before he entered the kitchen. "Your *vadder* told me to come right in. I hope that's *oll recht*."

"Why wouldn't it be?" Missy asked. She watched as Meg took a second bite of muffin. "Sit, Peter. Have a muffin, and I'll get you both a cup of tea."

Peter sat, and Meg shoved the plate in his direction. "Chocolate?" he asked, as he looked at what was left of her muffin.

"I love chocolate," she admitted with a smirk.

"I thought you preferred lemon," he said, reminding her of their banter over what kind of birthday cake they would order for the party.

She laughed. "I love chocolate *and* lemon."

"That makes it easier then, doesn't it? As I do, too."

"*Ja*, we'll have to order two cakes, one in each flavor. Can't have either parent feeling deprived," Meg said. Her mother set cups of tea before each of them. Meg thanked her, then gazed at Peter, who had taken the seat across the table from her. "You're here early."

"Am I?" he queried. "I don't remember arranging a time."

Meg frowned. "Ten. We said ten." She bit her lip. "'Tis only nine fifteen."

His lips twitched. "You want me to go and come back later?"

"*Nay*, I'm ready, or I will be after I've enjoyed another muffin and this cup of tea."

"Well, then *gut*." He ate his chocolate muffin and drank his tea.

When they were done eating and drinking, Meg grabbed her coat and followed Peter through the front door. He waited outside, ready to assist if necessary. It wasn't.

"Meg!" Her father crossed the yard. "Reuben left, then. That's *gut*. Peter, you'll show my *dochter* where she'll be going on Monday?"

"I will."

Arlin nodded with approval. "You'll be back afterward?"

"I thought I'd ask Peter to take me to the store while we're out and about." She hesitated, feeling sheepish. "Peter?"

"I'll bring her back after she shops, apparently."

Her father laughed. "Better you than me, Peter."

Peter was unusually quiet as he stood by while Meg climbed into the carriage, and then as he got in beside her. He steered his horse away from the house and onto the road in the direction of the physical therapy clinic. There was an edge of tension between them, and Meg tried to recall the moment it had crept in.

"Peter?"

He glanced at her.

"Is something wrong?"

"Nay." He sighed. "I'm just full. I ate too many of your *mudder's* muffins."

Meg stared at him and forced a smile. She didn't believe for one moment that having eaten too much was the reason for his silence. Their banter had been light as they'd enjoyed breakfast together. She thought about it and froze. It was after her father had mentioned Reuben's visit that Peter had grown especially quiet. She studied him unobtrusively. Why? Because he didn't care for Reuben as much as Reuben didn't care for him? Or was there another reason?

A tiny seed of hope blossomed in her heart. *Is it possible that Peter is jealous?*

Chapter Sixteen

It had been a good day. Peter had brought her home a half hour ago, and Meg was pleased with how many invitations they'd gotten done. They'd gone from house to house, personally inviting family and friends, starting with her aunt Katie, then moving on to visit each of Katie's married sons. It had been great to visit her cousins' homes. Every one of them was excited to be included in the party surprise, and as she'd thought, each of their spouses wanted to help with the food. After the Lapps, Peter had driven to the Amos Kings and the Abram Peachys. Both families were close friends of her *dat* and Peter's *mam*.

Tomorrow they planned to invite Peter's cousin Mary and her husband, Ethan. The Bontragers were newly-weds, having married the same week as Nell and James. They lived in New Holland, and Meg looked forward to the drive there. Mary was Sally's sister and the eldest daughter of Alta Hershberger. As their plan for tomorrow, Peter had assured her that Mary, like Sally, would have no trouble keeping news of the party from their mother. They would tell her a few days prior, not before, when it was too late for Alta to unleash the secret and ruin the surprise.

During their journey back, Peter had asked, "Are you going to invite Reuben?"

"Nay," she'd replied. There was no indication that the thought made him jealous. "If I did, I'd have to invite his family, and they don't know my *dat* or your *mam*. I think 'tis best to keep things simple. Don't you?" She'd heard him agree, then had dared to casually ask, "Will you be inviting Agnes?"

"Nay," he'd said, "for the same reason." And Meg had been relieved.

As she waited for Reuben's arrival, she realized that she looked forward to sharing with Peter the results of their hard work.

It was three o'clock. Reuben got off work at three thirty, he'd said, and he'd be coming here right afterward. Meg wandered into the kitchen, looking for her mother. Her *mam* stood by the stove, stirring a simmering pot. Whatever she was making for dinner smelled delicious. "Is that chicken and dumplings?"

"Ja." Her mother gave one last stir before she set down her spoon.

Meg moved closer for a peek. "My favorite." She closed her eyes as she sniffed.

Missy put on the teakettle. "How was your day?"

"Gut." She told her mother about the people Peter and she had invited, and their plans for the next day.

Her mother looked pleased. "'Tis coming together."

"Ja." Meg stood by the stove, enjoying the warmth of the kitchen and her mother's company. "Reuben will be here soon."

"You need a place to talk?"

Meg bobbed her head. "Where is everyone?"

"Ellie is out cleaning a house, and Charlie went with Leah to visit Nell." Missy took cups and saucers out of the cabinet, taking for granted that Meg wanted tea. "You can talk in the great room. 'Tis too cold outside for a walk."

"And I'm still wearing this brace, so I wouldn't want to go far," Meg added.

Forty-five minutes later, Reuben knocked on the back door. Meg rose to let him in.

"*Hallo*, Meg." His grin pierced her heart as she returned the greeting. She knew his happiness at seeing her wouldn't last for long.

He really was an attractive man, and right now she smelled the outdoors on him. He wore a navy knit hat, which he tugged off as he entered. As he removed his coat, she noticed he wore a long-sleeved blue shirt tucked into blue tri-blend denim pants held up by black suspenders. On his feet, he wore work boots. His blond hair was partly matted, while other strands were tousled from his cap. His cheeks, nose and ears were red, a good look on the man, who was not only kind, but thoughtful, too. Meg wondered why she couldn't love him as she should. Her thoughts raced to Peter. She knew why, but it didn't make her feel any less guilty for what she was about to say to Reuben.

"You're cold. Let me fix us tea, and we can take it into the other room." Her mother had gone outside to the barn to feed the animals. Meg longed for the day when she could take over the chore again.

She felt Reuben's gaze on her as she brewed two cups of tea, and he accepted one. He followed her into the great room and sat down. "You're looking well, Meg. Really *gut*. I'm so glad you're healing."

Meg experienced a rush of excitement as she told him about her leg. "I start physical therapy next week."

Reuben beamed. "Thanks be to *Gott*. You don't know how happy I am that you're *oll recht*." He reached across the distance between their chairs to grasp her hand.

Meg stifled the urge to jerk away. She waited a heartbeat before using the excuse of her tea to slowly withdraw, as if she needed both hands to hold her cup. "Reuben."

"Meg," he responded playfully.

Setting down her teacup, Meg sighed. "Reuben, I...I don't think we belong together. I like you, but it doesn't feel right."

He stiffened, and stared at her. "You're breaking up with me."

Meg saw disappointment in his blue eyes. "We weren't actually a couple, were we? You said you wanted to court me, but did I agree? *Nay*, I didn't."

"Meg—"

"I'm sorry, Reuben. I didn't want to hurt you." She regarded him with sadness, because she was causing him pain. *Better now than later*, her mother had said. Meg straightened in her chair. "I owe you a lot. You saved my life, and I thought to give us a chance because of it, but I just can't."

Reuben leaned back in his seat. "You don't owe me anything."

"But I do," she insisted. "You pulled me from the water. You saved me."

He was shaking his head. "I know the paramedics and EMTs said I saved you, but I didn't. I couldn't have." His lips firmed, and embarrassment flickered in his blue eyes. "I couldn't have saved you. I'm afraid of water. I can't swim."

Meg stared at him as his words registered. "You didn't save me?"

"Nay." He lifted a hand to run his fingers through his unruly hair.

"Then who did?"

"I didn't recall at first, but recently it came back to me. That night." He laughed. "Peter. It was Peter Zook. I remember seeing him. I heard his voice, asking if I was *oll recht*, telling me that you were right beside me and he was going to get us help." He glanced away. "Peter is the reason you don't want me."

"Reuben—" But she broke off as it hit her. Peter had saved her?

"Don't deny it, Meg. I've seen the way you look at him."

"He's with Agnes," she whispered, stunned by his certainty.

Reuben raised his eyebrows. "Are you sure?"

Meg nodded. *"Ja.* I know this."

"Maybe you should do something about that. Tell him how you feel. Meg, one thing I've learned since our accident is that life can be cut short in an instant." He studied her with affection. "'Tis fine, Meg. I'll be fine."

"I'm sorry."

"I can't know this for certain, but Peter—he sounded broken up when he spoke of you at the accident scene. He might care for you as you do him."

"Nay."

"You sound so sure."

"Ja." She gazed up at Reuben as he stood.

"I should go. I wish you all the best." He looked regretful. "I'm sorry I wasn't the one who kept you from drowning, Meg. I'm sorry I couldn't be the hero you wanted me to be."

Meg pushed herself upright. "You're a *gut* man, Reuben Miller. There is a woman out there for you. Not me, but someone else. Someone who'll love you as you deserve to be loved."

The tiny upward curve of his mouth only made his good looks better. "Take care of yourself, Meg."

She followed him to the door. "I won't forget how *gut* you were to me, Reuben. I know we probably can't be friends right now, but know that I'm here if you feel differently someday."

With a heart that ached for him, she watched him leave. As Reuben's buggy disappeared from sight, Meg tried to wrap her head around the fact that Peter had been the one to save her. He'd rescued her, but had never said a word.

Tears filled her eyes. "He didn't want me to think anything of it. He didn't want my gratitude. *He doesn't want me.*"

She had to work with him for only a little longer. After the party, she'd make sure he wasn't held to his offer of taking her to physical therapy. He had simply used the excuse so they could continue with the party planning.

Dare she tell Peter what she'd learned? What Reuben had told her?

"Nay," she whispered, as she slowly climbed the stairs to her room. If he'd wanted her to know, Peter would have told her himself. Yet her heart hurt, not for Reuben, but for herself.

It made sense now why Peter had come to visit her in the hospital. He'd said he wanted to see how she was faring. And she'd been startlingly polite as she tried to mend fences with a man who hadn't liked her. Then she'd learned that he actually *had* liked her, years ago…

and she'd felt better, until she remembered Agnes's role in Peter's life.

He'd wanted a friendly working relationship. What he didn't know was that he'd stolen Meg's heart.

Peter would be back for her tomorrow. Between now and then, she had to find the strength to pretend that she didn't know he'd been the one to rescue her. He would never learn about her feelings for him, and he'd never find out that she'd broken things off with Reuben.

But for now, Meg lay on her bed and had herself a good cry.

Meg was unusually quiet when Peter came for her the next day. Since they'd left her house, she'd given one-word replies whenever he'd asked her anything. "Think we can finish the invitations today?" he'd asked.

"Ja," she'd replied.

And the conversation had continued that way for the first mile, then two, until he'd become quiet himself. The silence was painful.

Peter frowned as they reached the Ethan Bontrager home. Would she act withdrawn while they spoke with his cousins?

He had his answer moments later. Meg came alive as she greeted Mary and Ethan and entered their house. He felt a painful tightening in his chest as he observed her. Apparently, she was silent and unhappy only with him. Why? Had he done something to upset her? She'd been fine yesterday, pleasant and smiling.

As they left the house with the Bontragers' promise to attend and continued to the next family on their list—the Adam Troyers—Peter opened his mouth to demand to know what was wrong. But then he shut it, realizing he didn't want to make matters between them worse.

After the Troyers, they visited Nell and James. Peter listened while Meg explained about the party to her eldest sister and her husband. Satisfied when they agreed to attend, she seemed less tense as they left.

"Meg?"

Her eyes dimmed as she met his gaze. *"Ja?"*

His heart tripped painfully. "Nothing." She frowned, and he said the first thing that came to mind. "Anyone else on our list?"

"Just the William Masts."

He inclined his head and drove in that direction. After a quick visit to the Masts, during which Meg again came alive and did all the talking, Peter took her home.

"I guess we've done all we can until we get closer to the party," he said.

"Ja." She studied her house as if eager to get inside.

Forlorn, he started to turn away, then paused. "Meg? What about Christmas decorations? Shouldn't we cut pine boughs and holly?"

She glanced at him, her expression hooded. *"Ja,* you're right. When?"

"Tomorrow?" he asked, hopeful that the tension between them would ease by then.

She nodded.

"I'll be by tomorrow morning at ten. We'll go over to the tree farm." He paused. "Will that be okay?"

She looked for a moment as if she would argue, but nodded instead. Then without another word, she went into the house, while he got into his buggy and departed.

The next day turned out to be a good one to cut Christmas greenery. They knew the owner of the farm, and he was willing to allow them their cuttings for a small fee. As they walked through the grounds, Peter prayed to see more enthusiasm from Meg. Again, she was too quiet, and he nearly demanded that she talk with him. So he prayed that whatever it was that bothered her, she'd be able to set it aside so they could continue to work together. He wanted his mother to have an enjoyable birthday party, a little bit of celebration to cheer her up after a rough year.

And he wanted him and Meg to be friends. Or maybe more.

"Are you sure we're not cutting too early?" Meg asked, after Peter had snipped off a few pine limbs.

"If they don't make it, we can always return for more," he said with a grin.

But she didn't smile back, so he made quick work of the cuttings, then took her home.

"I'll come for you on Monday to take you to physical therapy," he said, after he'd helped her from the carriage.

"Peter…"

"'Tis no trouble."

She nodded, then turned toward the house.

"Meg?"

He saw her stiffen before she faced him. *"Ja?"*

"Have a nice day."

He didn't know what to make of her weak, "You, too" in response.

Scolding himself for being all kinds of a fool, he drove to Agnes's house and invited her for a drive Monday afternoon. Meg's physical therapy was in the morning. He could make it to the Beiler home by two o'clock.

But Peter regretted the invitation he'd made to Agnes right after she'd accepted, because his thoughts remained with Meg.

Visiting Sunday rolled around, but Peter didn't go. He felt ill. He urged his parents to attend, said he knew how to reach them if he needed them. They'd be at the Abram Peachys, and he knew Meg would be there. He wasn't ready to see her. And he was sick—sick at heart, wondering what he should do about his feelings for Meg and his commitment to Agnes, which he was struggling with.

When his parents returned at the end of the day, Peter was at the kitchen table, trying to choke down a cup of tea. "Peter," his mother said. "Still not feeling well?"

"I'm getting there. Figured I should try to eat something with a cup of tea." He gestured toward the cracker box on the countertop across the room. He'd munched on a few saltines and felt better for doing so.

"Well, you don't have to worry about taking Meg to her physical therapy appointment tomorrow morning," his *dat* said. "Arlin wants to take her."

Peter knew he should feel relieved, not disappointed. But this was the last week before the party, and he and Meg had a lot to do. It would have been better to see her alone, on his own terms, to smooth things over so that they could work well together these next few days. "I can take her," he said, sincerely wanting to. "I'm feeling better already."

But Horseshoe Joe shook his head. "Arlin wants to see what Meg has to do. He's determined that she get the best care, and he said he needs to meet her physical therapist."

"Oh." Peter hid his disappointment.

"But he said you can take her on Tuesday."

He brightened. "*Gut* to know."

The next afternoon Peter went to get Agnes. It was a typical prewinter day, with temperatures in the low thirties. He'd brought an extra quilt and a thermos of the hot chocolate he knew Agnes liked.

She came out of the house as soon as he steered his horse into the yard.

"Hallo!" he called.

Her lips tilted, but the good humor didn't reach her eyes. Peter frowned. Was she feeling poorly?

He reached under his seat for the extra quilt and handed it to her. "It's chilly. Thought you'd like to stay warm." He gestured toward the back seat. "A thermos of hot chocolate, especially for you."

Her smile seemed more genuine as she covered her legs with the quilt. "That's kind of you, Peter, but I'm not thirsty right now."

"No Alice today?" he said conversationally, after a lengthy silence.

She stiffened. "Do you want to go back and get her?"

He glanced at her with surprise. *"Nay*, I wanted this time with you. Not your sister." He returned his attention to the road. "It's just that you usually like her to come with us."

He heard her sigh. *"Ja*, I usually do."

She was quiet, reflective, and he could tell something was wrong. "Agnes, what's bothering you?" he asked with a quick look in her direction. He saw her bite the inside of her cheek. The sound of her breath struck him as labored. "Agnes?"

"'Tis not working out between us, Peter. I liked that we were friends and I'd hoped for more, but it's not to be."

He saw a clearing on the side of the road near an old Amish cemetery. He pulled off the road and then turned to her. "What exactly are you saying, Agnes? That you don't want to be my friend? My sweetheart? What?"

Her eyes filled with tears. "You don't love me, Peter, and I don't love you. This will never work between us. We shouldn't deny our hearts and try to make something more from a simple friendship."

"Agnes—"

But she held up her hand. "Let me say what I have to say," she whispered. He nodded for her to go ahead. "Meg," she said. "You've cared for her, *loved* her, for a long time."

"Our families are friends—"

"There is someone else, Peter. I found someone that I might make a life with. I know where your heart lies and it's not with me. It's with Meg Stoltzfus." Her smile was sad. "You should tell her how you feel. She may have no idea. I watched her with Reuben. Doesn't look like she cares for him. I think she's trying to, but I don't think she's succeeding."

Peter stared at her, realizing the truth. "You've been a *gut* friend to me, Agnes. You deserve better than what I could have offered you. I hope whoever you've set your heart on is worthy of your love."

She reached for his hand. "I'll always have happy memories of our friendship, Peter, but I don't think we should see each other again. 'Tis easy enough when you're in one church district while I'm in another."

He agreed. "I'll take you home." As he turned the buggy and headed back, Peter listened to Agnes's happy chatter. It was as if, now unburdened, she'd returned to her old self. Yet he knew a moment's sadness. He would miss Agnes's bright smile and high spirits. She had always been able to put a grin on his face. But that was done. There would be only one way for him to feel happy, and that was if someday, somehow, Meg became a permanent part of his life, first as his sweetheart and then as his wife.

Do you care for Reuben, Meg? Or was Agnes right about her having feelings for him?

Do I have a chance of winning your heart if I confess how much I love you?

Chapter Seventeen

It was two days before Christmas. Meg was in Bishop John's house overseeing her sisters and three other community women, including Sally Hershberger and her sister, Mary Bontrager, as they cleaned to get ready for the Christmas holiday and the party the day after.

She hadn't seen Peter in over a week. He hadn't come to visiting day at the Peachys' and she'd sent word to him that she no longer needed for him to take her to her physical therapy appointments. Her father had taken her to her first appointment, and after that, the duty was passed from Leah to Nell, then finally to her mother. She was both glad and disappointed that she hadn't talked with him. Their last-minute plans were in the works. Meg had sent a message about the house-cleaning, and Peter had replied through Annie that he'd ordered the two birthday cakes from Maggie Mast's bakery.

The party was in three days, and then it would be over. She felt an underlying sadness that she and Peter would no longer have any reason to spend time together. Despite the hurt she'd felt upon learning that he'd kept his rescue of her a secret, she'd enjoyed the time they'd spent together as they planned their parents' party.

She wasn't wearing her brace today. Her physical therapy sessions had apparently already made a big difference in strengthening her calf muscles and foot. The party would be the first time that Peter would see her without the leg brace. Would he even care? She doubted it. Why should he care at all about her? He had Agnes.

"We've finished, Meg," Leah said, as she and Ellie came down the stairs.

"Me, too." She conveyed her thanks to all the women who'd helped today. Meg studied her surroundings. The great room looked festive, with holly branches and pine boughs set out to give the place a splash of Christmas cheer. The cuttings that she and Peter had gathered hadn't made it. So she'd told Eli to ask him to cut more, which he had.

Sally entered from the kitchen area. "I've put the food for tomorrow and Christmas in the bishop's pantry. He should have plenty to eat before we all descend on him for the party."

As if he heard his name, John Fisher came into the house from outside. "You've been busy," he said, as he noted the holly and pine.

"We hope you don't mind, but we did a little decorating," Meg said. Her Amish community didn't put up Christmas trees, but they did enjoy the greenery with bright red berries.

"Looks *gut*," he said gruffly.

Meg noticed that he'd lost some of the sadness in his eyes. When his gaze swept briefly toward Sally, she had an inkling the man felt a little something for the one woman who'd been there to help him whenever he'd needed her. "We should go and leave you in peace."

"Where's Nicholas?" Mary asked. "I haven't seen him since he was an infant."

"I'll check on him," Sally offered, and disappeared up the stairs.

No one moved. Sally returned downstairs moments later, carrying the bishop's adorable son.

"Ah, he's sweet," Mary cooed, and the women who were still there echoed her sentiments. "I want one like him." Mary's eyes warmed. "I'd like a lot of children."

Nicholas rested his head on Sally's shoulder, clearly at ease with the woman who held him, as if she were his mother. John gazed at Sally with his son, and Meg saw emotion shift in his expression. Longing. Warmth. Affection.

Meg experienced a longing of her own. She wanted children as well, but there'd be none if she couldn't have them with the man she loved. Peter.

She encouraged the others to leave. Only Sally lingered, to fix lunch for little Nicholas and his father.

Reuben had encouraged Meg to tell Peter she loved him. Could she do it? She didn't know. She could try to tell him at the party.

She had spent the last few weeks making Christmas gifts for her family, and birthday gifts for her father and Peter's mother. She had made a special thank-you present for Peter for helping her to plan the party. She would give it to him that night. She would act breezy, as if it was no big deal, but she had put a lot of love and hard work into the scarf she'd knitted for him.

She blinked back tears. It would be the last time she'd see him but for Sundays. Rarely would their paths cross during the week. "Foolish girl," she murmured. "Why did I have to fall in love with him again?" Or had she ever been out of love with him?

* * *

Her family spent Christmas together, just her parents, her sisters and Nell's husband, James. They exchanged gifts, and Meg was happy that everyone seemed to like the little presents she'd made for each of them. She knew how to sew. She and Martha—Eli's wife and a widow before her cousin had married her—had made craft items for the local fire company's mud sales. She'd attended a lot of them in past years, hoping to see Reuben, who sometimes worked as auctioneer. The sales auctioned off donations from Amish families, including quilts, furniture, farm equipment and small items like the pot holders, aprons and numerous other kitchen and household crafts that she and Martha had made and donated.

The family enjoyed a turkey dinner with all the fixings, including stuffing, cranberry sauce, green beans, mashed potatoes with gravy, dried corn casserole and apple pie with ice cream. They'd celebrated her father's birthday as they usually did, with a pan of lemon squares she'd made especially for him.

When her sisters decided to walk off the food outside, Meg followed. It had snowed during the night, a dusting that caused no travel issues and simply looked beautiful.

She loved walking without the restriction of the brace. She felt stronger every day. She'd been sleeping well at night, and her spirits had risen with the knowledge that the birthday party was tomorrow, and she would see Peter.

On the morning of Second Christmas, Meg and her sister Leah drove to Bishop John's for one last assessment of what else needed to be done. They had a lot of food in the back of their buggy. She and her mother and sisters had cooked and baked up a storm. Her aunt had brought her food contribution by as well—three vegetable dishes and a huge pan of chocolate fudge.

As she helped to carry everything inside, Meg couldn't help grinning as she thought of the fudge and Peter. He liked chocolate, and he said his mother preferred it over lemon, as well. Did that mean he would like the fudge more than the second pan of lemon squares she'd baked early that morning?

Everything was ready. She was doing a last check of the house when she heard a male voice in the kitchen. Meg headed that way, then froze on the threshold. Peter Zook had come with the two birthday cakes. He glanced up and saw her, and his eyes brightened. Suddenly, Meg was overwhelmed with joy. Tomorrow, things might be different, but tonight was for his mother and her father, and everyone would enjoy the evening because of the work they'd done together.

After placing the cakes out of sight in the bishop's pantry, Peter approached her. "*Hallo*, Meg." His expression was warm, and she felt a tingle from the top of her head to the bottom of her feet. "Looks like we're ready to go."

"*Ja,*" she breathed. "Everything looks *gut*. I see you picked up the cakes from Maggie's."

"Smelled delicious in there. It was nice of her to keep them in her bakery until we needed them. Nicer still that she opened up early so I could get them."

"I should get home before my *vadder* wonders where I am." She waved to Leah, who motioned that she'd be right there. Meg met Peter's gray eyes again. "I'll see you later."

"You will." He said it like a promise, and her heart thrilled at his tone.

* * *

The party guests arrived an hour before Meg and Peter's families. The Zooks and Stoltzfuses met up outside—prearranged by Peter and Meg—and walked up to the bishop's house together.

"I'm glad John is having guests. It must be lonely for him now that Catherine is gone," Miriam Zook said.

"But he must be coming around, if he's willing to have us all here, *ja*?" Meg raised her hand and knocked. She was overly aware of Peter's presence behind her, but didn't look back.

"*Ja*, that is encouraging. The man should marry again, if only to have a mother for that sweet little boy of his," Alta Hershberger said. She had come with the Zooks. Miriam, Peter's mother, was sister to Alta's late husband, John, the love of Alta's life. She made a sound of annoyance. "I don't know why Sally had to go with Mary and Ethan. She could have come with us."

Meg knocked again, and the door opened, revealing a smiling Sally, who held Nicholas in her arms. Alta blinked. "Sally—"

"Come in, *Mam*. Mary and Ethan are waiting inside. A few others are here to visit, as well." Sally blushed. "John has something important to tell everyone."

The families entered the house, hung up their coats and followed Sally to the great room. "You go first, *Dat*," Meg said.

At the same time, Peter urged, "*Mam*, you lead the way."

Miriam Zook and Arlin Stoltzfus entered the room just as everyone shouted, "Surprise! Happy birthday!"

Meg saw the stunned look on her father's face. She glanced at Miriam and witnessed her equally shocked expression.

"What's this?" she heard Alta exclaim. "Why didn't I know about this?"

Her daughters laughed. "Because we wanted to surprise them, *Mam*. If you'd known, then so would everyone else!" Mary said.

Alta looked momentarily offended, until Sally thrust little Nicholas into her arms. "Hold him, *Mam*. He's a sweetheart. Look how much he likes you."

Peter's aunt's face softened with joy. "What a precious *bubbel*!"

Meg exchanged happy glances with Peter. They had done well working together. They'd had their rough spots, she thought, but they'd gotten the job done.

Peter moved away to mingle with the guests. Meg stood by her father and mother, along with Horseshoe Joe and Miriam Zook.

"How did you do this?" Arlin asked his wife.

"Meg did it." Meg's *mam* eyed him with affection. "With Peter."

When her father regarded her with awe, Meg shrugged. "I had to do something while I was recuperating."

Alta approached, still holding Nicholas. "What a nice party," she said. Her daughters came up behind her. "Such a sweet boy." Alta rubbed her hand lovingly over the child's head. She flashed Mary a look. "When are you and Ethan going to give me a grandchild?"

Mary smirked. "In about seven months."

Alta gaped. "Did you say seven months?"

Ethan strolled up to place an arm around his wife. "*Ja.* You'll be a grandmother by next July."

To Meg's shock, tears filled the woman's eyes. "I…" She drew a sharp breath. *"Danki,"* she whispered.

Bishop John approached. "Sally," he said.

Sally inclined her head. "*Mam?* That precious little boy—he's to be your *kinskindt*, too. John has asked me to marry him."

Alta looked stunned. "You'll be marrying the bishop and Nicholas will be ours?"

John appeared amused. "*Ja*, but we'll be marrying soon. I want Sally in my life as soon as possible." His voice lowered as he eyed his bride-to-be with affection. "I never thought I'd feel this way again."

Meg placed a hand on Sally's arm. "I'm happy for you." She had guessed from the start about Sally's love for Bishop John. To know that John returned her feelings gave her hope that with the Lord's help, sometimes life turned out the way people wanted.

She loved Peter. She wanted to tell him. She had to tell him. If she didn't, she'd never know whether or not she could have had a life with him.

Moving away from the group, Meg went to look for him. She spied him in the other room, smiling, talking with…Agnes. Meg felt her stomach bottom out. He'd told her that he wouldn't invite her, but there she was, laughing with him. Agnes looked bright, happy. And Peter seemed pleased that she was there.

He suddenly caught sight of her, and his mouth started to curve. Meg spun, unable to bear the sight of the man she loved with the woman he wanted instead of her. She grabbed her coat and rushed outside. She needed to escape. Pain threatened to overwhelm her, to the point that she wanted to curl into a little ball and cry.

Meg stood outside, thinking hard. Was this the way to get over him? Would she allow Peter to take away any chances of her happiness? She stomped back inside, hung up her coat and sought out the attention of another man. She saw Nate Peachy in the corner, gazing about the room as he sipped a soda. She approached. "Nate."

He saw her and grinned. "Meg. Nice party."

She gave him a half smile. "I'm glad you could come."

Nate shrugged, his eyes perking up at the sight of Meg's sister Charlie as she crossed the room to talk with a group of young people. "I remember the time your sister climbed into my father's pigpen. Charlie wanted to pet the pigs, but all she got was her dress covered in mud and a hard nudge from our sow."

Meg laughed, imagining the scene. "She's fearless."

He grinned. "She is."

Charlie left the others to grab food from a table across the room. Nate was quiet as he watched her. Realizing that she'd lost his attention, Meg eased away, observing as he moved in Charlie's direction. Her sister lifted her head and met his gaze. She stiffened and quickly escaped, with Nate following.

Meg felt deep heartache as she watched them. Would she ever have someone who loved her enough to want to marry her?

With tears threatening, she found her coat again and hurried back outside. She'd couldn't bear watching Nate and Charlie. She couldn't stand watching Peter and Agnes.

The blast of cold air caught her by surprise. It was as if the wind had picked up in the moments since she'd been inside. Now it taunted her, made her shiver, and she once more wanted to cry. She leaned against the front porch railing and stared at the night sky. Would she ever get over Peter? Would the pain ever go away, or would she be destined to hurt like this forever?

* * *

"You came with Daniel," Peter said. He studied Alice Beiler, noted her pleasure in the company she was keeping.

"Ja," she said. "I like him. We only met recently, and we got along from the start. When he asked me to come, I couldn't say *nay."*

Peter understood. He listened while Alice told him how she and Daniel had met, all the while searching the room for Meg. He'd caught her glance earlier. He'd been happy to see her gazing at him, until she'd turned abruptly and left the room.

"Alice, there's something I have to do," he said after their conversation had continued for a bit. "Will you excuse me?"

Alice merely smiled. Daniel had come to stand beside her, and her focus was on him.

Eager to find her, Peter went looking for Meg. The memory of Agnes's words rang in his ears. *You should tell her how you feel.*

He had to talk with her, tell her how much he loved her. He smiled. Give her the Christmas gift he'd arranged for her with the help of her family—Honey, the little dog they'd rescued.

Peter caught sight of her parents in the kitchen with his. "Have you seen Meg?"

Arlin frowned. *"Nay.* She's not in the other room?"

"Maybe she escaped outside for a breath of fresh air," his mother suggested.

Peter thanked her and said he'd check. He moved to where the coats were hung in the front of the house. He donned his woolen jacket and went outside. He didn't have to go far. He immediately saw her by the porch railing, bathed in moonlight. The sight of her stole his breath. Warmth and love rushed through him as he moved to her side.

"Meg." He heard her gasp, saw her shoulders stiffen. "It's just me," he told her. "Peter."

She turned slowly, and he saw tears shimmering in her eyes.

"What's wrong?" He shifted closer and slipped his arm around her. "Talk to me. Why are you crying?"

"'Tis nothing."

He scowled. "Doesn't seem like nothing." He hesitated. "Meg, I need to talk with you. I know we're done with the party planning, but there is no reason we can't stop seeing each other. I can take you to your physical therapy sessions. We can go out to lunch—"

"Nay." Refusing to meet his gaze, she stared out into the yard. "I don't think that would be wise, do you?" She paused. "Agnes is *gut* for you. We'll see each other at church gatherings, but otherwise, it would be best if someone else took me for my physical therapy."

"Meg…" he objected.

"Go back into the house, Peter. Please leave me alone. I don't want to see you right now."

He inhaled sharply as pain squeezed his heart. He went blindly inside. She didn't want him. He'd hoped, but now he knew she didn't care for him at all. He stumbled into the great room, caught Reuben's and Meg's names mentioned in the conversation between her sisters and his cousins. He hung back and shamelessly eavesdropped.

"Meg broke it off with Reuben," Ellie was saying. "No surprise there, when she's loved Peter for as long as she's known him. But will she tell him? *Nay.* Sometimes I think I'd like to knock some sense into her."

Peter's heart started to thrum. Meg loved him? And

she'd broken off her relationship with Reuben? Then why had she chased him away?

She'd mentioned Agnes. He should have spoken up and told her that they were no longer seeing each other.

He froze. *Alice.* She must have thought he'd been talking with Agnes, had invited her to the party when he'd told her he wouldn't.

His pulse started to race with hope. He turned, rushed to grab his coat, and slipped it on before he opened the door to confront Meg on the front porch. "Meg."

But the space was empty. There was no sign of her anywhere. Calling her name, he ran out into the yard. "Meg! *Meg!* Where are you? Please, Lord, tell me where she went."

The wind picked up, a gust chilling him to the bone. She'd need to get warm. He stared at the bishop's barn and prayed that she'd headed in that direction. He sprinted to the outbuilding, slid open the barn door and slipped inside. "Meg!"

There was no answer. But he knew if she was upset with him, there was every likelihood that she'd pretend she wasn't there.

And then he heard it. A soft, heartfelt sob, one Peter would know anywhere. Meg was crying somewhere in the building. He saw a faint glow of light, hurried in that direction and found her in an empty stall. She was huddled in the straw with a flashlight to keep the dark at bay, shivering, crying.

"Oh, Meg," he murmured, as he slipped inside the stable to be with her. He hunkered down beside her. She gasped, startled, when he reached out, placed a finger beneath her chin and lifted her face to meet his gaze. "How can I help you?"

She inhaled sharply and stared. "What are you doing here, Peter?"

"I love you, Meg Stoltzfus. You—not Agnes. Agnes and I broke up. She knew—has always known—that my feelings for you would never go away."

"But you invited Agnes." Still, there was a glimmer of hope in her gaze.

"*Nay*, I didn't. You saw me talking with Alice, her twin sister. She came with your cousin Daniel. He invited her to the party."

Meg blinked, and he enjoyed the way her thick dark eyelashes swept down, then rose as she peered up at him. Using his finger, Peter caressed her cheek. "Meg, will you be my sweetheart? Will you allow me to court you? I want to court, then marry you. Will you give me a chance? I've loved you for so long. Please, Meg. Be my girl."

Meg started to cry harder.

Concerned, Peter could only stare at her. "I'm sorry," he muttered. "I thought—"

"You rescued me," she said, as her tears continued to fall. "And you didn't tell me." She sniffed. "Why didn't you tell me?"

"You were with Reuben. You wanted him. It didn't matter who rescued you, only that you were saved." He tenderly cupped her face, then wiped away her tears with his thumbs.

"You love me?" When he nodded, she quieted and straightened away from the barn wall. As she studied him, Peter saw her blue eyes fill with longing and love…and joy. She lifted a hand to cover his fingers and cradled them against her cheek. "I wanted you to be happy, even if it was with Agnes."

"I never loved her as I do you." He kissed her forehead. "Will you be my girl?"

In the flashlight's golden glow, her face lit up like sunshine. "*Ja*, I'd like that." She bit her lip. "Peter, I love you."

His heart sang out with joy as he stood and gently eased her up to stand beside him. "I never thought I'd have you. You're all I've wanted for so long."

"I am?"

He gave her a smile. "*Ja*. I fell for you from the first moment I laid eyes on you. I couldn't stop looking at you. I couldn't stop staring."

Her breath came out in a shaky laugh. "I thought you stared because you found something lacking in me, especially after what I overheard."

"*Nay*, sweetheart. *Nay!* Never that."

She shot him a look of loving affection. "Thank you, Lord," she murmured.

Peter pulled her into his arms. "Amen." After a hug, he released her and reached for her hand. "'Tis cold here. Let's go inside and get warm."

Meg beamed at him as they walked together toward the house.

Epilogue

The weather was unseasonably warm for November. The crops were harvested, and it was the time for weddings. Dressed in her new light blue dress, Meg sat next to Peter in the front row of the congregation in her aunt and uncle's great room. She glanced over at her bridegroom with a ready smile. Her heart tripped. Peter wore his black Sunday best, and she'd never known a more handsome and loving man.

As if sensing her regard, he met her gaze, his gray eyes dark and filled with emotion. They had waited eleven long months for this day, and both of them were eager for this moment when they would start their lives as man and wife. He loved her, and Meg had never been happier.

Meg's day had begun at four o'clock this morning, when the family had taken care of their daily chores. Later, at six thirty, women from the community had arrived to help prepare the house and ready the wedding feast. The wedding ceremony would be held at her aunt Katie's before everyone came to enjoy the celebration.

At the start of the three-hour service, while the church community members had sang hymns, Meg and

Peter were drawn aside by Preacher Levi, who counseled them in another room. Then the bride and groom returned to the service in time for a prayer, scriptures and a long sermon.

As she paid attention to the preacher's words, she felt Peter's fingers entwine with hers. He gave them a squeeze, and when she looked at him, she saw a small smile curve his lips as he continued to gaze ahead.

Their wedding party sat nearby—Nell and James, Annie and Meg's cousin Jacob, Josiah with his wife, Nancy, and her other Lapp married cousins, Eli, Noah and Jedidiah, with their wives.

Preacher Levi called Peter and Meg to the front of the gathering room. He asked them to tell them what their marriage was to be, then he blessed them. Bishop John Fisher and Deacon Abram Peachy joined them, along with other church members, to give testimony about their marriage.

To everyone's delighted surprise, Meg's mother and Horseshoe Joe stood and told everyone that they'd known about their children's love for each other for years and had shared a hand in giving them a little push. Meg gazed at Peter in shock. His lips twitched as he contained his laughter. She grinned back.

A final prayer concluded the ceremony, and the newly wedded couple climbed into a waiting buggy, driven by Josiah. Soon they were back at the Arlin Stoltzfus house for the wedding feast. As Peter and Meg took their seats in the *Eck*, the honored place in the corner of the room for the bride and groom and their wedding party, invited guests sat at tables set up as a U shape in the room. Settling at Peter's left, Meg thought of all the wonderful things her husband had done and continued to do for her. He was always showering her with kindness and affection. She smiled. He did the same for her dog, Honey, whom he cared for as much as she did.

"How are you feeling, wife?" Peter whispered as he leaned close. His breath was a soft puff of air in her ear.

"I'm feeling happy, husband." Her gaze lingered on Peter's handsome face, her heart filled with all the love she felt for him. They would be living in the main Zook farmhouse. His father and mother already had moved into the *dawdi haus* on the property, the house where Peter's grandparents once had lived.

"You're not sorry to be married to me, are you?"

Startled, she could only stare, her pulse fluttering. "*Nay*, are you?"

"Never." His smile warmed her like the rays of a summer sun. He caressed her cheek, then leaned in to kiss her properly, on the lips. "Wife," he murmured. "I love you, Meg Zook."

She sighed dreamily. Peter was her Christmas blessing, one that had continued throughout the past year and would forever. "As I love you, Peter Zook, forever and for always until death do us part—" she paused and reached under the table for his hand "—and into the next life."

* * * * *

Dear Reader,

Welcome to the Amish village of Happiness and the Women of Lancaster County. Meg Stoltzfus, sister of Nell, whose romance was told in *A Secret Amish Love*, has met her match in Peter Zook. The two have never gotten along despite the fact that each had feelings for the other at one time or another. Meg is involved with Reuben Miller, a man she wanted since she met him two years ago, while Peter has moved on from his feelings for Meg to pursue a relationship with Agnes Beiler.

But fate steps in to cause Meg and Peter problems when they are forced to plan a surprise party for Meg's father and Peter's mother together. They must learn to work amicably and get along, a tough thing to do when each of them has been hurt by the other.

I hope you enjoy Meg and Peter's Christmas love story and that you will return with me on future visits to Amish country in Lancaster County, Pennsylvania, as we witness other women of Lancaster County struggle with the men in their lives. May God keep you and hold you in His loving hands.

Blessings and light,
Rebecca Kertz

AN AMISH ARRANGEMENT
Amish Hearts • by Jo Ann Brown

Hoping to make his dream of owning a farm come true, Jeremiah Stoltzfus clashes with Mercy Bamberger, who believes the land belongs to her. When Mercy becomes foster mom to a young boy who only Jeremiah seems to reach, suddenly their mission becomes clear. But will their hearts open for each other?

THE TEXAN'S TWINS
Lone Star Legacy • by Jolene Navarro

Reid McAllister is surprised to find the wildlife sanctuary where he's doing community service is run by Danica Bergmann, the wife he left behind—and that he's the father of twin daughters he didn't know he had! Now he's determined to help Danica keep her dream alive—and earn her trust in their family's happiness.

CLAIMING HER COWBOY
Big Heart Ranch • by Tina Radcliffe

Jackson Harris never thought investigating Big Heart Ranch's claim to be a haven for orphaned children would turn him into a temporary cowboy—or that he'd be falling for adorable triplets and the ranch director! Lucy Maxwell's plan to put the city lawyer through the wringer also goes awry as she's roped in by his charm and caring ways.

A MOM FOR HIS DAUGHTER
by Jean C. Gordon

Discovering she has a niece who's been adopted, Fiona Bryce seeks to get to know the little girl. Widowed single dad Marc Delacroix isn't sure he can trust that Fiona won't seek custody. Neither imagined that caring for three-year-old Stella would lead to a chance at a forever family.

HER HANDYMAN HERO
Home to Dover • by Lorraine Beatty

Reid Blackthorn promised his brother he'd keep an eye on his niece—so he takes a job as handyman with Lily's guardian. Tori Montgomery hired Reid to help with repairs to her B and B, never expecting she'd develop feelings for him. But can their relationship survive when she discovers his secret?

INSTANT FAMILY
by Donna Gartshore

Single mom Frankie Munro is looking for a fresh start—she has no time for romance. But when she and her daughter rent a lakeside cottage, next-door neighbor Ben Cedar makes it difficult to stick to those plans. As neighbors turn to friends, will camaraderie turn to love?

Get 2 Free Books,
Plus 2 Free Gifts—
just for trying the Reader Service!

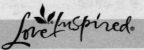
Jeremiah looked up to see a ladder wobbling. A dark-haired woman stood at the very top, her arms windmilling.

He leaped into the small room as she fell. After years of being tossed shocks of corn and hay bales, he caught her easily. He jumped out of the way, holding her to him as the ladder crashed to the linoleum floor.

"Are you okay?" he asked. His heart had slammed against his chest when he saw her teetering.

"I'm fine."

"Who are you?" he asked at the same time she did.

"I'm Jeremiah Stoltzfus," he answered. "You are…?"

"Mercy Bamberger."

"Bamberger? Like Rudy Bamberger?"

"Yes. Do you know my grandfather?"

Well, that explained who she was and why she was in the house.

"He invited me to come and look around."

She shook her head. "I don't understand why."

"Didn't he tell you he's selling me his farm?"

"No!"

"I'm sorry to take you by surprise," he said gently, "but I'll be closing the day after tomorrow."

"Impossible! The farm's not for sale."

"Why don't you get your *grossdawdi*, and we'll settle this?"

"I can't."

"Why not?"

She blinked back sudden tears. "Because he's dead."

"Rudy is dead?"

"Yes. It was a massive heart attack. He was buried the day before yesterday."

"I'm sorry," Jeremiah said with sincerity.

"Grandpa Rudy told me the farm would be mine after he passed away."

"Then why would he sign a purchase agreement with me?"

"But my grandfather died," she whispered. "Doesn't that change things?"

"I don't know. I'm not sure what we should do," he said.

"Me, either. However, you need to know I'm not going to relinquish my family's farm to you or anyone else."

"But—"

"We moved in a couple of days ago. We're not giving it up." She crossed her arms over her chest. "It's our home."

Don't miss
AN AMISH ARRANGEMENT
by Jo Ann Brown, available January 2018 wherever
Love Inspired® books and ebooks are sold.

www.LoveInspired.com

LIEXP1217

Love Inspired®

Inspirational Romance to Warm Your Heart and Soul

Join our social communities to connect with other readers who share your love!

Sign up for the Love Inspired newsletter at **www.LoveInspired.com** to be the first to find out about upcoming titles, special promotions and exclusive content.

CONNECT WITH US AT:

Harlequin.com/Community

 Facebook.com/LoveInspiredBooks

Twitter.com/LoveInspiredBks

LISOCIAL2017

SPECIAL EXCERPT FROM

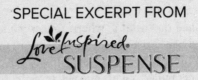

Love Inspired.
SUSPENSE

*Special Agent Tanner Wilson has only one clue to figure
out who left a baby at the Houston FBI office—his
ex-girlfriend's name written on a scrap of paper.
But Macy Mills doesn't recognize the little girl that
someone's determined to abduct at any cost.*

Read on for a sneak preview of
THE BABY ASSIGNMENT *by Christy Barritt,*
available January 2018 from Love Inspired Suspense!

Suddenly, Macy stood. "Do you smell that, Tanner?"

Smoke. There was a fire somewhere. Close.

"Go get Addie," he barked. "Now!"

Macy flew up the steps, urgency nipping at her heels.

Where there was smoke, there was fire. Wasn't that
the saying?

Somehow, she instinctively knew that those words
were the truth. Whoever had set this fire had done it on
purpose. They wanted to push Tanner, Macy and Addie
outside. Into harm. Into a trap.

As she climbed higher, she spotted the flames. They
licked the edges of the house, already beginning to
consume it.

Despite the heat around her, ice formed in her gut.

She scooped up Addie, hating to wake the infant when
she was sleeping so peacefully.

Macy had to move fast.

She rushed downstairs, where Tanner waited for her. He grabbed her arm and ushered her toward the door.

Flames licked the walls now, slowly devouring the house. Tanner pulled out his gun and turned toward Macy.

She could hardly breathe. Just then, Addie awoke with a cry.

The poor baby. She had no idea what was going on. She didn't deserve this.

Tanner kept his arm around her and Addie.

"Let's do this," he said. His voice held no room for argument.

He opened the door. Flames licked their way inside.

Macy gasped as the edges of the fire felt dangerously close. She pulled Addie tightly to her chest, determined to protect the baby at all costs.

She held her breath as they slipped outside and rushed to the car. There was no car seat. There hadn't been time.

Instead, Macy continued to hold Addie close to her chest, trying to shield her from any incoming danger or threats. She lifted a quick prayer.

Please help us.

As Tanner started the car, a bullet shattered the window.

Don't miss
THE BABY ASSIGNMENT by Christy Barritt,
available January 2018 wherever
Love Inspired® Suspense books and ebooks are sold.

www.LoveInspired.com